Charles S. Bradley, Rhode Island General Assembly

The Methods of Changing the Constitutions of the States

especially that of Rhode Island

Charles S. Bradley, Rhode Island General Assembly

The Methods of Changing the Constitutions of the States
especially that of Rhode Island

ISBN/EAN: 9783337381165

Printed in Europe, USA, Canada, Australia, Japan

Cover: Foto ©Andreas Hilbeck / pixelio.de

More available books at **www.hansebooks.com**

THE METHODS

OF CHANGING THE

CONSTITUTIONS OF THE STATES,

ESPECIALLY THAT OF

RHODE ISLAND.

———•———

BOSTON:
ALFRED MUDGE & SON, PRINTERS,
No. 24 FRANKLIN STREET.
1885.

CONTENTS.

AN ARTICLE ON CONSTITUTIONAL REFORM. — SOME SUGGESTIONS CONCERNING A RECENT OPINION OF THE SUPREME COURT OF RHODE ISLAND.

Providence Journal, May 31, 1883.

I.

To the Editor of the Journal:

The right of the people of the State of Rhode Island to adopt a new constitution in place of the present one, by the method heretofore adopted in this and all the States of the American Union, has recently been denied. That method is, through a convention of delegates, called and elected by the people, to frame a new constitution, and the acceptance of that constitution by a vote of the people, the whole proceeding being with the approval and pursuant to an Act of the Legislature of the existing government. This denial is found in the report of a majority of a committee of the General Assembly, and in an opinion of the judges of the Supreme Court. The latter opinion was given in answer to two inquiries of the Senate of the State. The second was as follows, viz. : "As to whether it is legally competent for the General Assembly to submit to the qualified electors the question whether said electors will call a convention to frame a new constitution, and to provide by law, if a majority of the electors voting upon said question shall vote in favor of calling such convention, that the same be held, and the new constitution framed by said convention be submitted to the electors for their adoption, either to the electors qualified by law, or to the persons who may be qualified to vote under such new constitution, and whether, if a majority of the electors or persons voting thereon vote for the adoption of such constitution, whether the constitution, so to be framed and adopted, would be the legal constitution of the State, and, as such, be binding on all the people thereof?" The first is substantially the same, except that the convention is supposed to be assembled by an act of the Legislature, without vote of the people, they electing the delegates but not calling the convention.

The Court answer, " That the mode provided in the constitution for the amendment thereof is the only mode in which it can be constitutionally amended," and that "any act of the Assembly providing for a convention to amend the constitution is unconstitutional and void." The ground upon which the denial rests is, that the provision for amendment in the constitution by acts of legislation and votes of the people inferentially precludes all other modes of change.

This is the usual mode of amendment by the acts of two Legislatures, an intervening special publication, and the vote of the people. It is found in not less than forty of the State constitutions adopted in this country. It existed in all the constitutions submitted to the people of Rhode Island previously ; the question, therefore, is not a new one in the constitutional history of the States of this country. The denial is novel. As the paramount question of American public law, it challenges the attention and consideration of the people of this State.

A construction has also been put upon the opinion of the judges, that it is like a judgment to which, whether right or wrong, parties must submit ; that it is binding upon the action of other departments of the government, and obligatory upon all the citizens of the State.

That these new doctrines of constitutional law should be thus declared is partly explicable by the peculiar circumstances under which the opinion of the judges was given. The inquiry was made on the 24th of March, the opinion given on the 30th, when the Assembly adjourned over election week for ten days on the 30th. The election was held on the 4th of April. The subject of constitutional reform was before the people in the election. No action was taken upon the opinion by the Assembly, except that upon its reception it was ordered to be placed on file and printed. These circumstances should be borne in mind in considering the opinion. And the Court say : "The questions are extremely important, and we should have been glad of an opportunity to give them a more careful study ; but under the request of the Senate for our opinion 'without any unnecessary delay,' we have thought it to be our duty to return our opinion as soon as we could, without neglecting other duties, to prepare it." As the legitimate purpose of calling for such opinion is in aid of the action of the Legislature, and as such action was not possible until after the ten days' recess for the election, and as it is the right of the Court to determine what response it will make, and at what time, to such request, it is to be regretted that more time, at least, was not taken by the Court. The opinion, however, must be, and has been, taken as it is, and its reasoning and its conclusions considered as they are, as no modification of it has been suggested.

II.

The construction of the opinion that it is binding upon the other departments of the State and the citizens is one for which the opinion itself may not be alone responsible. That conclusion is derived from it in the able summary of the opinion in the editorial columns of the *Journal*. It is considered also in other editorial columns that the opinion is an insuperable barrier to any attempt by a law of the General Assembly to provide for the calling of a constitutional convention and the election of delegates thereto by the people, and the preparation and submission of changes in the constitution by the convention to the people, and the adoption by them of these changes. Such a law, the opinion declares, would be "unconstitutional and void."

This opinion of the Court is not like a judgment, binding upon the parties before it, whether right or wrong. It is simply an opinion of these judges who signed it, carrying no force of obligation with it. For this is a subject upon which a court cannot sit, even in independent judgment. The political branch of the government is the determining power upon questions of this nature. Upon these questions it is the duty of the judicial department to follow and sustain the decisions of the other departments. What is the legitimate constitution of a state, and who are its magistrates, is decided by the political department. The consciences and judgment officially expressed of officers of that department are the appointed authorities upon these questions. The Court is their creation, and must yield obedience on this subject to them. It is not their creator, and over their action it has no mandatory power in this regard. It is strange that in Rhode Island this doctrine should be doubted or denied. For in this State it has been officially declared by its Supreme Court in an important constitutional trial, that of Thomas Wilson Dorr. The prisoner in that case offered evidence of the proceedings which he claimed show him to be the constitutional governor of the State at the time of the acts charged, and therefore exercising lawful power.

The Court say in their charge: "This evidence we have ruled out. Courts and juries, gentlemen, do not count votes to determine whether a constitution has been adopted or a governor elected or not. Courts take notice, without proof offered from the bar, what the constitution is or was, and who is or was the governor of their own State. It belongs to the Legislature to exercise this high duty. It is the Legislature which, in the exercise of its delegated sovereignty, counts the votes and declares whether a constitution be adopted or a governor elected or not, and we cannot revive or reverse their acts in this particular, without usurping their power. And why not? Because if we did so we should cease to be a mere judicial, and become a political, tribunal, with the whole sovereignty in our hand; neither the people nor the Legislature would be sovereign; we should be sovereign, or you would be sovereign." "Sovereignty is above courts and juries, and the creature cannot sit in judgment upon its creator." The admirable statement of the principle that on this subject "in this particular," if the Legislature pronounces a government to be constitutional and valid, it is not in the power of its courts to pronounce such government unconstitutional and void, was quoted in full by Mr. Webster, in his argument of the Rhode Island case, Luther v. Borden, before the Supreme Court. That Court gave upon this point a unanimous judgment, and refer to the "clear and forcible" opinion of the Supreme Court of Rhode Island, in the trial of Dorr.

That Court further said: "The question which the plaintiff proposed to raised by the testimony he has offered has not heretofore been recognized as a judicial one in any of the State courts." "The political department has always determined whether the proposed constitution or amendment was ratified or not, by the people of the State; and the judicial power has followed its decisions." Referring to the Rhode Island decisions, the Supreme Court of the United States further say: "But the Court uniformly held that the inquiry proposed to be made belonged to the political power, and not to the judicial; that it rested with the political power to decide whether the charter government had been displaced or not; and when that decision was made, the judicial department would be bound to take notice of it as the paramount law of the State." And again: "If it (a court) decides at all as a court, it necessarily affirms the existence and authority of the government under which it is exercising a judicial power."

It is an entire misconception as to the power and position of a court to suppose that it can direct the action of any of the political officers of the government, or of its citizens, in determining in such cases what is and what is not the lawful government of a State. Such attempts, our philosophic chief justice of the olden time of our constitution said, in behalf of the court, would be a usurpation.

Such is the present law, as shown by recent decisions. White v. Hart, 13 Wallace, 646, was a case before the United States Supreme Court in which the validity of the constitution of the State of Georgia was denied. The Court said, "The action of Congress upon the subject cannot be inquired into. This case is clearly one in which the judicial is bound to follow the action of the political department of the government, and is concluded by it."

III.

We will proceed to consider the opinion with all the respect due to the high source from which it emanates, and inquire whether it is in harmony with the constitutional law of the States of this Union, and especially with that of this State. This question of the power of the people over their constitution has well been called the most important question of American public law. It is a question upon which the experience of all the States, our own included, has shed a flood of light, and we need not err, unless we disregard that experience, and steer away into the outer darkness of merely individual opinions. Mr. Webster, when pleading the cause of our State before the Supreme Court of the United States, in conjunction with one of our own citizens, Mr. John Whipple, worthy to be his colleague, will command our respect as an expounder of constitutional law. That argument he himself chose to submit as his opinion and judgment on this question of American constitutional law to posterity, in the last volume of his works, dedicated to the memory of his beloved daughter, and that of his youngest son, who gave his life to his country in the war with Mexico. Mr. Webster sums up the American constitutional law upon the right of the people to change their constitutions in the following terms : " We see, therefore, from the commencement of the government under which we live down to this late act of the State of New York, one uniform current of law, of precedent, and of practice, all going to establish the point that changes in government are to be brought about by the will of the people assembled under such legislative provisions as may be necessary to ascertain that will, truly and authentically."

The act of the State of New York thus quoted by Mr. Webster, and which he had dwelt upon in detail as an illustration of American constitutional law, was an act of legislation providing for a constitutional convention under an existing constitution, containing a provision for amendment through a majority vote of one Legislature, followed by publication and a two-thirds vote of the next Legislature, and a majority vote of the people. It contained no provision for calling a convention, and no declaration of rights upon the subject. Our constitution provides for amendment by a majority vote of one Legislature, followed by publication, a majority vote of the next Legislature, and a three-fifths vote of the people. This proceeding in New York, Mr. Webster takes as typical of American constitutional law, of the American method of changing a constitution.

The act of New York to which Mr. Webster referred he thus describes : " One of the most recent laws for taking the will of the people, in any State, is the law of 1845, of the State of New York. It begins by recommending to the people to assemble in their several election districts, and proceed to vote for delegates to a convention. If you will take pains to read that act, it will be seen that New York regarded it as an ordinary exercise of legislative power. It applies all the penalties for fraudulent voting, as in other elections. It punishes false oaths, as in other cases, certificates of the proper officers were to be held conclusive, and the will of the people was, in this respect, collected essentially in the same manner, supervised by the same officers, under the same guards against force and fraud, collusion and misrepresentation, as are usual in voting for State or United States officers."

We thus see that the identical proceeding which the report and opinion pronounce unconstitutional and void, Mr. Webster, the expounder of American constitutional law, standing in the Supreme Court of the United States, the chosen representative, the advocate and defender of Rhode Island, takes as his illustration, and declares it to be in conformity with the uniform current of American law, precedent, and practice. The report referred to this argument, and quoted in italics Mr. Webster's opinion, that the people may in their constitutions put restrictions upon their own action. That is not the question now in issue. The present question is whether the American provisions for legislative amendment of a constitution is a prohibition of their power to change a constitution through the medium of a convention, and by a vote of the people, acting under the sanction and safeguards of an ordinary act of legislation which calls for a convention and provides for its action. There were no special provisions of the constitution of New York directly or indirectly sustaining the action of the Legislature, convention, or people, which Mr. Webster nevertheless approved. He speaks of such acts with approval, as acts of ordinary legislation. In our constitution there are two special provisions, either of which would fully sustain an affirmative answer to the inquiry of the honorable Senate. There are many instances in the history of the country similar in every respect to those of New York. There are none in accordance with a denial of this right of constitutional reform.

IV.

To look further at the subject historically : When the independence of the United States was achieved, the sovereignty before existing in the Crown or Parliament of Great Britain was transferred to the people of the States. He who argues for this proposition, argues, Mr. Webster says, without an adversary. In exercising this sovereignty in making or unmaking constitutions, the people cannot assemble in mass ; they must assemble by delegates, who will consider and propose a constitution and submit it to the people to be adopted or rejected. Nearly all our constitutions have thus been adopted in this country. Perhaps as many rejected. The common-sense of this method is obvious. The same common-sense, the same practical wisdom in the affairs of government, has adopted a provision for those partial and occasional amendments for which the assembling of a convention is inexpedient or unnecessary. This is through the action of the Legislature, usually, from caution, of two Legislatures, with an intermediate and special publication to call the attention of the people to the subject, and then a vote of the people. These two methods exist side by side in many constitutions which have been adopted in this country. The latter method cannot exist without a special provision for it in the constitution. The former, as the opinion of our court admits, may exist without such special provision for it. It is inherent in the system of popular sovereignty. Constitutions have been adopted through the action of conventions, assembled pursuant to a law of the existing Legislature, in almost all the cases, if not all in which constitutions have been created or renewed. And this, whether the constitution contained a special provision for calling a convention or not, and also whether it contained a provision for legislative amendment or not, and whether the latter stood alone in the constitution or with a provision for a convention. As the cases where the constitution did not contain provision for amendment or for a convention are admitted to be cases in which conventions can assemble, we will not consider them ; but only those in which the court think such convention and acts of legislation cannot constitutionally exist because of the provision for legislative amendment. And of these also, we will omit the many where a special provision for a convention exists, and consider those only where such provision for legislative amendment stands alone. There are many such in the history of the country. And though the opinion says, "it is inconceivable to us that they" (*i. e.*, our ancestors) "would have elaborated so guarded a mode of amendment, unless they had intended to have it exclusive and controlling," the action of jurists, statesmen, and people, in many and leading States, is in direct conflict with this opinion. What history shows to be conceivable and possible in other States, under the same circumstances, should be, of course, conceivable and possible in Rhode Island.

In Massachusetts, the constitution contained a provision for an amendment by a majority of the Senate and two thirds of the House in one Legislature, publication, and the same vote in the next Legislature, and then a vote of the people.

It is stated in the opinion that "one of the greatest of modern jurists, Chief Justice Shaw, was of the same way of thinking" (as themselves), "and conjointly with his associates declared it to be his opinion that the constitution of Massachusetts was constitutionally amendable only as therein provided." As this is the only reference made by our Court to any other opinion upon this subject, it should be carefully examined. This opinion was given without argument or discussion of the questions involved. Upon examination of the opinion, it is by no means clear that the judges meant to express an opinion that the acts of a convention elected by the people at the instance of the Legislature would be unconstitutional and void. On the contrary, they seem to recognize the validity of such proceeding.

The two questions addressed to the Massachusetts Court were unlike the two questions submitted to our Court. Our judges are asked if a constitution framed through a convention and act of legislation by the people would be binding upon the people. The first question in Massachusetts assumes the validity of a constitution framed through such convention of delegates, and only asks if the convention would be limited to the specified parts of the constitution proposed for alteration in the act of the Legislature and in the vote of the people calling the convention. The Court answer that the convention would be thus limited.

So the second question asks merely whether the "specific and particular amendments" provided for in their provision for legislative amendments can be made otherwise than as thus provided. To answer this question the Court are careful to say that they do not give an opinion as to what would be "the effect of any change or alteration of their constitution, made under such circumstances, and sanctioned by the assent of the people," that is, circumstances "of great emergency, or upon the obvious failure of their existing constitution to accomplish the object for which it was designed." They do not say that such change or alteration would not be binding, but decline to give any opinion upon that question, which is substantially the present inquiry.

They go on to consider the question as one in regard to "the rights and powers *derived* from and under the constitution and law," not the rights and powers *reserved* under the constitution. If the judges mean that under the derived powers there was no legislative special and particular amendment, except that provided in the constitution, they were in accord with the legislative and judicial mind of the country. If they meant more, if their answers are not to be construed in the light of the questions addressed to them, if they meant to be of the same way of thinking as our Court, they have not been so understood in Massachusetts, or at all events, have not been sustained by the jurists, statesmen, and people of that State.

Under this constitution a convention was assembled in Massachusetts in 1853. In that convention, Marcus Morton, who was one of the judges who gave the opinion, and who was twice governor of the State, said : "Whether we sit legally or illegally, whether by right or usurpation, if the people choose to adopt what we submit to them, it then becomes authority."

Joel Parker, a former chief justice of New Hampshire, who, in his judicial controversy with Judge Story, in regard to a question under the bankrupt law, was sustained by the Supreme

Court of the United States, was at that time Dean of the Law School at Cambridge, and a member of the convention. He said : " It is well known that the argument has been advanced (not opinion announced) that this convention was revolutionary in its character because the constitution provided no such mode in which a convention could legally assemble ; that there was one mode provided by the constitution for the revision of that instrument, and any other mode is in its nature revolutionary. For myself, personally, I do not entertain that opinion. I believe this convention to have been lawfully assembled, and that it is bound to proceed according to law."

Rufus Choate, the friend of Webster, said : " Assuming that the Legislature, which, by the act of May 7, 1852, ordained that this sealed envelope should be used in voting for delegates to the convention, had power under the constitution to make such a provision, as *in my judgment it is perfectly clear that they had, and which nobody has yet called in question.*"

The leading men of the State, of all schools in politics, were, as a rule, members of the convention ; and not one, it is believed, expressed a doubt as to the validity and constitutionality of the proceeding.

The people, by a close vote, rejected the proposed constitution : but not on the ground of the nature of its origin.

The case of New York has already been stated. The provision for amendment to the constitution of 1821 was the same as our own. Under it a convention assembled in 1845, and a constitution was adopted. Charles O'Connor, Samuel J. Tilden, Samuel Nelson, chief justice of the State, Ira Harris, also a chief justice, and others, their compeers, were members of the convention. One may well conjecture what would be the reply of such men as O'Connor, whose position as head of the bar was due not less to his conscientious and Christian character than to his abilities and learning, and the many like him throughout the country who have concurred in such conventions in States where the provision for amendment was the same as our own, to the imputation in the report that such men are revolutionists, and acted in violation of their oaths of office. Possibly they might answer to the able jurist in the committee, its chairman, that it was as much revolutionary and in violation of the oath of office to deny to the people and their Legislature the powers given them under a constitution, as it was to enlarge those powers beyond the constitution. Perhaps the expressive word Mr. O'Connor frequently used would escape from his curled lips. Probably the vast crowd of jurists, statesmen, and intelligent people would move on, little heeding this imputation, unless another trouble in Rhode Island might demand their attention.

The constitution of Pennsylvania, of 1838, contained the provisions for amendment by the vote of two succeeding Legislatures, special publication intervening, and then a vote of the people. It contained no provision for calling a convention. The Bill of Rights affirmed the right of the people to alter, reform, or abolish their government in such manner as they may think proper. A convention was called in 1873, pursuant to a legislative act and vote of the people. And the new constitution proposed by the convention was adopted by the people and went into operation. The Supreme Court, in a cause (Wells v. Bain, 75 Penn. St. 39) argued before it by the present attorney-general of the United States and by other eminent counsel, considered this subject. In their opinion the Court say: "The words in such manner as they think proper in the Declaration of Rights embrace but three known recognized modes by which the whole people of the State can give their consent to an alteration of an existing lawful form of government, viz.: First, the mode provided in the existing constitution. Second, a law as to the instrumental means of raising the body for revision and conveying to it the power of the people. Third, a revolution." "The government gives its consent either by pursuing the modes provided in the constitution or by passing a law to call a convention."

"It is not pretended that the late convention sat as a revolutionary body, or in defiance of the existing government, and it did not proceed in the mode provided for amendment in the constitution, that being a legislative proceeding only. It was, therefore, the offspring of *law*. It had no other source of existence. The process was an application or petition to the Legislature to call a convention; the passage of a law to gather the

sense of the people on the *question* whether a convention should
be called ; an election authorized by this law, to take the sense
of the whole people on this question ; and, finally, the passage
of a law to call the convention and define its powers and duties,
as law is the only form in which the Legislature, the body in-
vested with the powers of government, can act, and thereby its
own consent be given and revolution avoided."

The constitution of Missouri, of 1821, provided for an amendment by a vote of two thirds of two Legislatures, with an intervening publication. There was no provision for calling a
convention. The Bill of Rights affirmed the right of the people to alter their constitution, whenever necessary for their safety
and happiness. Under this constitution two conventions have
been called, in 1845 and 1865. The constitution proposed in
1846 was rejected ; that in 1865 was adopted.

In Louisiana the constitution of 1845 contained the usual
provision for legislative amendment by two Legislatures, with
a publication, and by a vote of the people. There was no provision in regard to a convention. The Declaration of Rights
contained no assertion of the power of the people to alter the
constitution. In 1852, a convention assembled in accordance
with an act of the Legislature and vote of the people, and the
constitution proposed by it was adopted. This constitution contained the same provisions, excepting the vote of the second
Legislature. Under it, and the reconstruction acts of Congress,
a convention assembled in 1864, and framed the present constitution, adopted by the people.

The constitution of Arkansas, of 1868, contained the usual
provision for legislative amendments, by two Legislatures, with
special publication and vote of the people, and no provision for
calling a convention. The Bill of Rights affirmed the right of
the people to alter the government whenever the public good
may require it. Under that constitution a convention was
called in 1864, and the present constitution adopted.

The constitution of 1868, in Texas, contained the usual provision for amendments by a two-thirds vote of two Legislatures,
a majority of the vote of the people, and publication intervening. It contained no provision for calling a convention, and

the Bill of Rights contained no claim of right in the people to alter the constitution. In 1876 a convention was called by the Legislature, and the constitution proposed by it was accepted by the people.

The constitution of 1834 of Tennessee contained the usual provision for amendment, a majority of one Legislature, two thirds of the next Legislature, and a majority of the popular vote. It contained no provision for a convention. Its Bill of Rights affirmed the right of the people to alter the government as they may think proper. A convention was called in 1870, and the constitution proposed by it was adopted.

The constitution of Mississippi, of 1832, contained the provision for amendment, omitting the act of the second Legislature. Under this, and the reconstruction acts of Congress, a convention was held and framed a constitution, which was adopted by the people in 1868.

The constitution of Alabama contained the usual provisions for legislation by two Legislatures, publication intervening, and the vote of the people. The majority in the Legislature must be two thirds. The Declaration of Rights affirmed the right of the people to alter, etc., the government in such a manner as they may think expedient. There was no provision in the constitution for calling a convention. The Supreme Court of Alabama, Collier v. Ferguson, 24 Ala. 108, in considering the validity of certain amendments under the constitution, say: "The constitution can be amended in but two ways, either by the people who originally framed it, or in the mode prescribed by the instrument itself. We entertain no doubt that to change the constitution in any other mode than by a convention, every requisition which is demanded by the instrument itself must be observed."

There may be other instances of States whose constitutions contain legislative amendment provisions standing alone, as it is claimed that it does in our own, where conventions have been held and constitutions adopted, in which the courts have expressed judgments affirming the right, like those we have cited. We know of none in which a contrary opinion has been declared in judgment, or acted upon by the people of a State.

Upon this question, whether the people of this country consider that the legislative methods of amendment exclude the action of the people through conventions, the fact that in more constitutions which have from time to time been adopted than there are now States, there are, side by side with the legistative method, a recognition of, or provision for, the convention method, would seem conclusive. In how many other constitutions which have been rejected the same fact existed, it is not easy to ascertain. Thus much for the opinion in the States as to the coexistence of the two methods, in express terms and by the action of the States.

Let us see what the action of the general government has been on the subject.

When changes became necessary in the constitutions of the States which attempted to secede, Congress provided that the ante-bellum constitutions should be changed through the medium of conventions, and not according to the method provided in them for amendment through the Legislature. That could as easily have been adopted as the other. It never seems to have occurred to these jurists and statesmen that any other mode than that provided in the constitution to be changed would be unconstitutional and void, upon the principles of American constitutional law. The States of Alabama, Arkansas, Georgia, Louisiana, Mississippi, Tennessee, and Texas had in their constitutions preceding the war the same provisions for amendment that we have in Rhode Island, without any provisions for a convention. And the proper method of change under them was deemed in Congress, and in those States, to be by convention, and not by legislative amendment.

Indeed, the "current of law, precedent and practice" has been running deeper and broader since Mr. Webster's time, and though individuals, jurists and laymen, may have dissented, it is believed that no official body has denied his doctrine except in our State.

We may be pardoned for quoting Webster upon what is the vital question, whether the power over our forms of government is in the government or people. In his reply to Mr. Calhoun, in 1883, he said: "The sovereignty of government is an idea

4

belonging to the other side of the Atlantic. No such thing is known in North America; her governments are all limited. In Europe, sovereignty is of feudal origin, and imports no more than the state of the sovereign. It comprises his rights, duties, exemptions, prerogatives, and powers. But with us all power is with the people. They alone are sovereign, and they erect what governments they please, and confer upon such powers as they please. None of these governments are sovereign in the European sense of the word, all being restrained by written constitutions."

It has been said by a court, in rendering judgment in a State whose constitution is, in this regard, the same as our own (Stowe, J., Wood's appeal, 75 Penn. St. 49): "The question whether the calling of a constitutional convention was a legal exercise of power by the Legislature should now be considered by all judicial tribunals as settled so firmly as a part of the common law of our government, that any attempt to disturb it would savor more of revolution than legitimacy."

V.

We leave the historic view of the subject, and proceed to briefly consider the legal reasoning upon which the opinion and report rest. The rule of law relied upon is stated to be that "where power is given to do a thing in a particular way, then the affirmative words marking out the particular way prohibit all others by implication, so that the particular way is the only way in which the power can be legally exercised." The Court further says: "We do not see why it (the rule) is not as trustworthy a guide to the meaning, when the language so used occurs in a state constitution, as when it occurs in a statute or a will."

This rule does not apply to provisions in a statute, so as to take away any right of the sovereign power.

"The rights of the crown can never be taken away by doubtful words or ambiguous expressions, but only by express terms." —Dwarris on Statutes, 706. The good sense of this qualification is manifest. Any legislation which is to affect the sovereign power should not leave the right to mere inference. It should be direct, especially in constitutions addressed to the popular mind and adopted by it; a great sovereign right should not be left to legal conjecture and implication. The people, in such proceedings, say what they mean. They do not leave a negation of one power to be inferred from the grant of another. The rule does not apply, again, in a statute so as to take away a right previously existing under the common law, or by custom, or by a preceding statute. It applies only to statutes by which all the rights claimed under it are granted by it. "Affirmative words do not take away the common law, a former custom, or a preceding statute."— Dwarris, 712.

The right here in question exists by the common laws of the constitutions of American States, as we have seen by the former customs of this and other States. It exists, also, as we shall see, by the enactment of this constitution. A grant of land to Indians by the government, with certain power of disposition, may be thus construed to determine the power of the Indians, hardly to determine the present or past powers of the government. A grant to a corporation, in its charter of power, to secure its debts in one way, does not, it has been decided, impliedly take away its power to secure them in another way. Thus much for the rule in case of statutes. It is said in the New York Court of Appeals, 4 Selden, 493, "The maxim, *Expressio unius est exclusio alterius*, is more applicable to deeds and contracts than to a constitution, and requires great caution in its application, in all cases." But we are dealing in larger subjects. Let us try to understand what a State constitution is in this regard. We say State constitution, for the minds of learned men in America are sometimes warped by a familiarity with the rule in the constitution of the United States, which is the reverse of the rule of construction in a State constitution.

Mr. Webster says, in his letter to the Barings, Vol. VI. of his works : —

"Every State is an independent, sovereign, political community, except in so far as certain powers, which it might otherwise have exercised, have been conferred on a general government, established under a written constitution, and exercising its authority over the people of all the States. This general government is a limited government. Its powers are specific and enumerated. All powers not conferred on it still remain with the States or with the people. The State Legislatures, on the other hand, possess all usual and ordinary powers of government, subject to any limitations which may be imposed by their own constitutions, and with the exception, as I have said, of the operation on those powers of the constitution of the United States."

That the power to pass an act providing for a convention of the people of a State to reconstruct their State constitution exists in the Legislature of a State, unless it has been prohibited, no one will dispute. It need not be specifically granted. It exists by force of this creation, or in grant to one branch of the government of general legislative power. The Legislature of our State has that power, unless prohibited, as a part of its prerogative and right ; not *ex-necessitate*, as the opinion says. There is, therefore, no room for any implied prohibition, for there is an express grant of the power in question by a general grant of legislative powers, which include it.

The rule does not apply, for the further reason, that the power granted and power in question are different. We have seen, historically, that the power to reconstruct a constitution and the power to amend are different. As they are in common understanding, the power to repair a house is different from the power to tear down and rebuild it. The power in a legislature to amend an act of legislation does not exclude the power to repeal the act and make a new one. So the power in a government to amend its constitution, as occasion may require, does not exclude the power to reconstruct it anew, as occasion may require. The meaning of language is determined by usage. The usage of the provisions and terms by the people of this country is certainly uniform and fixed. The suggestion that we use them in a different sense in Rhode Island has no perceptible foundation. Indeed, it is hardly affirmed in the report or opinion.

There is a difference in the legal status of these methods. The courts which maintain that they can sit in judgment upon the action of the Legislature in the exercise of its power of legislative amendments of the constitution, admit that this power of change through constitutional conventions is one in which the Legislature is above their control. In the most recent of those cases (in Iowa, Roehler *v*. Hill), the Court say, as to the argument of counsel, that they could not "decide that the constitution of 1857, under which they are organized, had not been properly adopted. The courts of this State possess no such power, and they could not assume such a jurisdiction. The reason why a court could not enter upon the determination as to the validity of a constitution under which it is itself organized is forcibly set forth in the case of Luther *v*. Borden, upon which appellant relies. The distinction between such a case and one involving merely an amendment not in any manner pertaining to the judicial authorities, must at once be apparent to the legal mind. The authorities recognize the distinction."

VI.

In conclusion, we will briefly consider some facts in the history of Rhode Island, and especially the special provisions of the constitution, which place beyond all doubt the right to change her constitution by the convention method.

The same provision for amendment which exists in the present constitution is found in each of the three constitutions before submitted to the people, — that of 1834, the people's constitution, and the landholders', so called. The proportion of the vote required to constitute a constitutional majority varies, but the plan is substantially the same. Is it to be presumed that those who voted for the people's constitution, and those who framed it, intended to deny the right to change a constitution by convention and popular vote? And many more votes were given for that than for the present constitution. We are not comparing the legality of the two constitutions, but citing the usage of this language among the people of the State.

The question, finally, in Rhode Island, in 1841 and 1842, was, whether a constitutional convention and vote of the people in adopting a constitution must be authenticated by an act of legislation, and have the concurrence of the existing government, to be constitutional and valid. That question was determined by the political department, and by the courts. It was brought into the convention that framed the present constitution by a proposal to adopt in the Bill of Rights the provision of the people's constitution. The matter was referred to a committee, and the present provision of the Bill of Rights was recommended and adopted in the following terms : —

SECTION 1. In the words of the father of his country, we declare : "That the basis of our political systems is the right of the people to make and alter their constitutions of government ; but that the constitution which at any time exists, till changed by an explicit and authentic act of the whole people, is sacredly obligatory upon all."

The first article of the constitution declares that the essential and unquestionable rights and principles hereinafter mentioned shall be established, maintained, and preserved, and shall be of paramount obligation in all legislative, judicial, and executive proceedings. Of these rights and principles the very first named is the right to alter their system of government by the explicit and authentic act of the people.

Now, there can be no doubt that a change adopted in the method pointed out by Mr. Webster, in his argument for the present government, and by the will of the people, assembled under such legislative provisions as may be necessary to ascertain that will truly and authentically, is an explicit and authentic act of the whole people.

No one will have the hardihood to deny that the act by which, throughout more than a century, the constitutions of the States of this Union have been made and unmade, is an explicit and authentic act for that purpose. None will so insult the character of Washington as to assume that in the use of that phrase in his farewell address he did not refer to that mode of change which he had so often witnessed around him, the only methods known at that time. This provision of our constitution is conclusive as to the existence of the right. It is not referred to in these denials of the right.

There is another provision of the constitution which grants

the power in question. Under the charter government, the General Assembly possessed all powers. Many of the people of the State preferred this patriarchal government to the division of powers systematically arranged in the usual State constitution. They yielded reluctantly to the pressure and persuasion of enemies and friends. While granting a constitution, they yet incorporate in it the provision that the General Assembly shall continue to exercise the powers they have hitherto exercised unless prohibited by the constitution. Among those powers was that of calling a constitutional convention. Had they meant to have excluded that power, they would have said so.

The mere permission to the Assembly to propose amendments does not prohibit the other power. It is said that there can be an implied prohibition. Taylor v. Place is cited for this doctrine. The principle there acted upon is thus stated: "Affirmative words, vesting power under a constitution, are construed as prohibiting the exercise of the power by all other departments of the government, tribunals, or officers, as the case may be, when otherwise the words would have no operation at all, or would not have their *full* and *proper* operation." In Marbury v. Madison, the case referred to, Marshall, C. J., said in this case: "A negative or exclusive sense must be given to them, or they have no operation at all." It certainly cannot be claimed that the amendatory power given to the General Assembly cannot operate or exist while the reforming power over their constitution by the people, through a convention and act of Assembly, also exists. The coexistence of these powers has been manifested in terms and in action under nearly fifty State constitutions in this country.

There are three provisions of our constitution by which these rights are secured to the people in the Assembly. First, the general grant of legislative power, which we have seen includes this power; second, the express reservation of the entire right of the whole proceeding in the first section of that Bill of Rights, which is declared to be of paramount obligation upon all departments of the governments; and third, the express provision that the General Assembly shall continue to exercise the powers they have hitherto exercised unless prohibited in this constitution.

There can be no implied prohibition under the rule relied upon in the opinion and report, because the rule only applies, by its very terms, to methods and powers not expressed. The Latin expressions of the rule in words that have been so anglicized as to be intelligible to all, express the rule with brevity and clearness : —

Expressio unius exclusio alterius expressum facit cessare tacitum.

The expression of one method is the exclusion of the alternative method not expressed. The express causes the tacit (unexpressed) to cease.

The whole argument for prohibition in our constitution rests upon the assumption that the power is nowhere expressed or reserved. This assumption is manifestly unfounded. The importance of the subject, not only in the present but in the long future, requires a full consideration of the legal and constitutional right.

A single word, in conclusion, upon the practical question. The Legislature represents localities ; the convention, the mind and character of the whole, and its varied interests. This very question of the present local distribution of power is one most requiring consideration.

When the late Judge Potter introduced a plan for a distribution of power, Mr. Simmons, the leading mind of the convention, said, "that according to this plan a small minority of the people of the State might elect every officer of the State. Thirty-six thousand people could elect as many senators and representatives as seventy-two thousand. This is the most arbitrary plan that ever was proposed, and which no one could defend before the enlightened citizens of the State. It was worse than the old system, and worse than any system which had been devised among civilized men for a republican government."

The system that was adopted has become worse than that so vigorously condemned. Now nineteen towns, containing thirty-six thousand three hundred and twenty-nine (36,329) people, elect a majority of the Senate. Thirty towns, containing ninety-four thousand nine hundred and seventy-two (94,972) people, elect a majority of the House. The total population of the State by the same census, 1880, was two hundred and seventy-six (276,531) thousand. This disproportion is constantly increasing. Is it just and right? If not, can it be wise? In this connection, it should be remembered there is no veto power in the governor, who represents the whole people of the State. This disproportion and injustice is constantly increasing.

Again, the independence of the judiciary is of primary importance. Under the present constitution, the seat of judge may be declared vacant at the annual session for the election of public officers, without hearing and without cause assigned, by the vote of a majority of those elected to the Assembly. But this is not the time to point out the provisions of the present constitution which are most injurious in their consequences to the best interests of the State. We have been considering the method of constitutional reforms.

A REPLY TO A PAMPHLET ENTITLED "SOME THOUGHTS ON THE CONSTITUTION OF RHODE ISLAND, BY THOMAS DURFEE," NOVEMBER, 1884.

A PAMPHLET entitled "Some Thoughts on the Constitution of Rhode Island, by Thomas Durfee," has recently appeared. The author is the chief justice of Rhode Island.

It discusses three of the proposed changes in the constitution which have somewhat occupied the public mind. To these twenty-four pages are devoted. The remaining pages, thirty-three out of fifty-seven of the pamphlet, purport to be a reply to an article published in the Providence *Journal*, in May, 1883, as to the methods of constitutional reform in Rhode Island.

The pamphlet opens with a eulogium upon Rhode Island, instancing especially the increase of the past thirty years in her wealth and population and in her facilities for education. It dwells upon the many virtues which characterize her people. From this eulogium there is no dissent. It also indulges in a eulogium of the makers of the constitution, or rather an attack upon some unknown persons by whom it says they have been "flippantly maligned." It further truly states that our constitution was the work of the law and order party, though but one of the five Democrats, Elisha R. Potter, whom it enumerates as the prominent men in the Democratic element of that party, and but one of the six Whigs, James F. Simmons, whom it enumerates as the prominent men in that element of the party, were present at the convention.

The pertinency of arguments drawn from the prosperity of the State as to the wisdom or unwisdom of the proposed amendments to which the author objects, would be illustrated if we could suppose that the chief justice of Massachusetts should issue a pamphlet in favor of the provision of the constitution of that State which makes no discrimination against foreign-born voters, and should instance in support of his argument, the increase of that State in wealth, population, and educational facilities, or should compare the much greater ratio of Fall River with that of Providence.

The provision in our constitution restricting the right of suffrage in naturalized citizens, which the pamphlet desires to uphold, is one not referred to in the article which it attacks. It is certainly a purely political question. The author of the pamphlet says, "I propose to look at a purely political question from a political point of view." The consideration, therefore, of this subject with which he occupies eighteen pages may be left to those political gentlemen who have charge of our interests in the General Assembly. That body has, during the past year, voted to propose an amendment of the constitution in that regard. The vote was well-nigh unanimous. But two fifths of the popular vote has heretofore defeated all amendments in regard to suffrage.

The second proposed change mentioned in the pamphlet relates to the ratio of representation in the Senate and in the House. The present representation in the House is based on the ratio of population in each town, with the limitation that no city or town shall have more than one sixth of the members of the House, whose number shall never exceed seventy-two, and that each town shall have at least one member; in the Senate there is one member for each town or city.

The author of the pamphlet says, "I do not think it would be unreasonable for her (Providence) to have a little larger representation, though personally I do not care for it." She has one senator and twelve representatives. Her population is 104,857, and the total population of the State is 276,531. The figures are those of the United States Census of 1880. It may be added that there are twelve towns, — one third of the entire number, — neither of which has a population of two thousand, and the average of which is about thirteen hundred; that three towns and cities, one twelfth of the entire number, have more than half the entire population of the State; and that five towns and cities have three fifths of the entire population.

The pamphlet charges that others, who also think that a change should be made, wish the Senate put on a strictly popular basis. Such is not the fact.

The life-long senator from Rhode Island, in his elaborate defence of Rhode Island,* made no attempt to defend the apportionment of political power under the present constitution.

A system less unequal than the present one has become was denounced in unmeasured terms by the leader of the convention that framed the constitution,† and was rejected by the body whose members are so highly eulogized in the pamphlet.

Never before in the history of the State or in any constitution proposed for adoption were senators elected by towns; still less was there any such ratio as at present.

And it must be noticed that the evil is increasing. The city of Providence has, by the action of the General Assembly, been greatly enlarged in area and population taken from the adjacent towns, and several country towns have been divided.

The third proposed change is the abolition of the registry tax. As to that the author of the pamphlet says: "I have long been of the opinion that the tax, by its perversion, has become a prolific source of evil. I have voted, and am ready to vote again, for its abolition. But while I condemn the tax, I cannot condemn the authors of it." So of the three proposed changes discussed by the author of the pamphlet, one to which he is opposed has already been recommended by the well-nigh unanimous vote of the General Assembly; to the other two he gives his sanction. He further says, "Amendments are also suggested, some of which I should not be sorry to see adopted, if they were constitutionally adopted." As he does not say what they are, his fellow-citizens are not enlightened, except by the important fact that he is in favor of still further changes.

The pamphlet has also said that "certain high offices go almost as a matter of course to men who can make or secure large contributions to the necessary funds." No weightier reason can be given for change and reform.

---

* DEFENCE OF RHODE ISLAND. Speech by Henry B. Anthony in the Senate of the United States. February, 1881.

† "Thirty-six thousand people," said Mr. Simmons, "could elect as many senators and representatives as seventy-two thousand. This was the most arbitrary plan that ever was proposed, and which no one could defend before the enlightened citizens of the State. It was worse than the old system, and worse than any system which had been devised among civilized men for a republican government." — *Journal of the Convention, September, 1842, p. 41.*

THE MODES OF CHANGING THE CONSTITUTION.

The pamphlet next comes to its question whether " the mode
provided in the constitution is the only mode by which it can
be constitutionally amended." The discussion of this question
is the principal purpose of the pamphlet, though not indicated
in its title. Unlike the rest of the pamphlet, it contains much
that is novel to the public, and that demands a reply.

THE SPIRIT AND PURPOSE OF THE DISCUSSION ADOPTED IN THE PAMPHLET AND PROPOSED IN THE REPLY.

The author of the pamphlet would make the discussion in
terms, and in his treatment of it, a personal one. He says, " I
shall endeavor to be brief, and at the same time plain and
simple, so that everybody can understand what I say, and easily
judge whether it be sound or sophistical." The truth is the only
worthy object of any man's endeavor in this discussion. Especially should this be so in one holding the office of a judge ;
with him a reverence of the truth is first and last and all the
time an essential requisite. Without it judicial integrity cannot
exist ; without it the decisions of a judge binding upon his
fellow-citizens are not a true expression of their rights. In
reply to what the pamphlet terms its counter argument, the
present writer will take as the test the simple inquiry on every
point, What is the truth?

THE CIRCUMSTANCES UNDER WHICH THE OPINION OF THE JUDGES WAS PREPARED. THE GREAT CAUTION PROPER IN GIVING SUCH OPINIONS.

The discussion has a long personal preface. It begins as
follows : " Before I take up Judge Bradley's argument I have a
word to say in regard to certain preliminary strictures on the
judges, in which he has been pleased to indulge himself." He
further says, " Judge Bradley blames them for their expedition,
and infers that their opinion must have been given off-hand on
a question which was new to them, and that it may therefore be

regarded as precipitate and ill-advised. I care nothing for the censure, but I contravert the inference." What Judge Bradley did say was: "That the circumstances (to wit, those under which the opinion was given) should be borne in mind in considering the opinion." He also added: "It is to be regretted that more time at least was not taken by the Court." As the pamphlet says that "the judges, in their opinion, expressed a regret that they had not had an opportunity for a more careful study," an expression of such regret by a well-wisher of the Court is certainly permissible. That is all there is in the article of what the pamphlet calls strictures, blame, censure, and inferences. All the rest is a cold statement of fact; none of the statements there made are denied or in any manner gainsaid in the pamphlet. We quote the entire statement in the article, that the reader may compare it with the statement in the pamphlet:

"That these new doctrines of constitutional law should be thus declared, is partly explicable by the peculiar circumstances under which the opinion of the judges was given. The inquiry was made on the 24th of March, the opinion given on the 30th, when the Assembly adjourned over election week, for ten days. The election was held on the 4th of April. The subject of constitutional reform was before the people in the election. No action was taken upon the opinion by the Assembly, except that upon its reception it was ordered to be placed on file and printed. These circumstances should be borne in mind in considering the opinion. And the Court says: 'The questions are extremely important, and we should have been glad of an opportunity to give them a more careful study: but under the request of the Senate for our opinion, "without any unnecessary delay," we have thought it to be our duty to return our opinion as soon as we could, without neglecting other duties, prepare it.' As the legitimate purpose of calling for such opinion is in aid of the action of the Legislature, and as such action was not possible until after the ten days' recess for the election, and as it is the right of the Court to determine what response it will make, and at what time, to such request, it is to be regretted that more time, at least, was not taken by the Court. The opinion, however, must be, and has been, taken as it is, and its reasoning and its conclusions considered as they are, as no modification of it has been suggested."

The pamphlet adds two important facts that will deepen the regret felt by every intelligent friend of the Court: one, that the judges " were holding court all the while " during the six days between the request and the opinion ; and second, the statement of the want of previous study of this "extremely important question." "That to one of the judges, at least," the pamphlet says, "the question was not novel, though I had not given it any especial study." If he had considered that any of his colleagues were better prepared than himself, it is to be presumed that he would have said so. He says, " The question had been known to me ever since the time, more than thirty years ago," when I heard the late Chief Justice Greene characterize the proceedings " in amending the constitution of New York, through the medium of a convention without following the method prescribed in it," "as a species of Dorrism." "His remark sunk the more deeply into my mind, like a living seed for future germination."

Chief Justice Greene had great legal knowledge, and a judicial habit of mind, which it has been often the pleasure of the present writer to acknowledge, as the pamphlet observes. But his friends never claimed for him that he was a constitutional lawyer. He gave little attention to political affairs or questions.

Chief Justice Greene and his colleagues once gave an opinion upon a constitutional question, in answer to a request from the General Assembly. That opinion was described by the Supreme Court of the State, in Taylor v. Place, as follows : "The grounds of the conclusion destroy the reservation, or the grounds of the reservation destroy the conclusion. Whichever way, we can hardly believe that the learned judges were guilty of such an oversight. We are inclined to think that when they said that 'they did not mean to intimate the slightest doubt of the validity of certain acts,' they meant merely not to express an opinion." Much more of similar criticism is found in the judgment in the case to which the pamphlet often refers. Knowing the judgment of our Supreme Court upon this advisory opinion to the Assembly by the late Chief Justice Greene, our present chief justice chooses to adopt, as a correct exposition of an "extremely important question" of constitutional law, his conversational remarks, instead of the concurrent judgment of the luminaries of the bar and bench, and of the eminent statesmen of both parties throughout the country. From such a conversation comes the seed, which, after lying in the fallow soil of a mind more than thirty years, germinates with little study or reflection (upon a question necessarily involving learning and research and historical inquiries from sources difficult of access and collection) into the opinion, and thence by a sequence natural to some minds into the pamphlet.

A further fact, not mentioned in the article, may be stated. That the election pending at the time of the opinion involved, in addition to the question of constitutional changes (if one may credit the Providence *Journal*, the morning reading of the chief justice), the continuance in office of some of the judges of the court. William Sprague was at that time the candidate of two conventions for governor. The action of the chief justice in regard to the Sprague litigation will hereafter appear in reply to other portions of the pamphlet.

The pamphlet claims that the judges are the constitutional advisers of the Assembly; it does not claim that it is within their province to issue an opinion on the eve of an election, as constitutional advisers of the people, at too late a period for reply, and such intent is not to be presumed.

The object of this provision of the constitution, as stated by Chief Justice Gray and his associates (122 Mass. 600), "is to enable the advice of the judges to be obtained upon any important question of law which the body making the inquiry has occasion to consider in the exercise of the legislative or executive powers intrusted to it." And even with this limitation, this provision, adopted by Maine, New Hampshire, and Rhode Island from Massachusetts, the only States in which it is believed that it exists,* has not worked satisfactorily, as the con-

---

* A similar provision, first introduced in the Missouri constitution of 1865, restricted to questions of constitutional law, was dropped, in framing the existing constitution of 1875.

clusions of the judges in these cases, unlike their judgment in ordinary cases, are not given after hearing adverse argumentative discussion; and hence the necessity of great caution in the exercise of the power.

The opinion of the Massashusetts convention of 1820, in regard to this power, is thus expressed in their " Address to the People": " In the second article of the third chapter it is provided that each branch of the Legislature, as well as the governor and council, shall have authority to require the opinion of the judges on important questions of law and upon solemn occasions. We think this provision ought not to be a part of the constitution; because, *First*, each department ought to act on its own responsibility. *Second*, judges may be called on to give opinions on subjects which may afterwards be drawn into judicial examination before them, by contending parties. *Third*, no opinion ought to be formed and expressed, by any judicial officer, affecting the interest of any citizen, but upon full hearing, according to law. *Fourth*, if the question proposed should be of a public nature, it will be likely to partake of a political character; and it highly concerns the people that judicial officers should not be involved in political or party discussions."

The constitution proposed by the convention in Massachusetts in 1853 prohibited the exercise of this power. It was not contained in any of the constitutions heretofore proposed in Rhode Island. The reader will find an instructive paper in regard to this provision whereby the judges can be called upon to give advisory opinions, in the Appendix. It is from the pen of Professor Thayer, of the Harvard Law School.

THE NATURE OF AN ADVISORY OPINION OF THE JUDGES UPON A POLITICAL QUESTION NOT LIKE A JUDGMENT OF THE COURT.

The author of the pamphlet says: "Judge Bradley next passes to a labored effort to show that the opinion of the judges is nothing but their opinion, and that the General Assembly has the same power to call a constitutional convention which it had before it was given. He professes to think that the judges themselves have somewhere advanced an exorbitant claim of authority for their opinions, though he confesses that they are not the chief offenders. I think the notion that they have offended at all is simply the coinage of his own too lively fancy. The only case that I know of in which the matter is so much as broached is Taylor v. Place, 4 R. I., 324, 330. The question there was, whether the General Assembly has judicial power, and the position was taken that the question was answered by the opinion of the judges, given at the request of the General Assembly, on the constitutionality of an act to reverse and annul the judgment for treason against Thomas W. Dorr, and was, therefore, to be regarded as *res adjudicata*. This position, however, was taken, not by the court, nor by any of the judges, but by counsel, and *mirabile dictu*, Judge Bradley was himself the counsel. Judge Bradley now distinguishes between a judgment of court and an opinion of the judges. He professes great reverence for the judges when deciding cases, but thinks they are entitled to no more respect than so many lawyers when they give an opinion. Doubtless his distinction is not unfounded, but, nevertheless, I think he pushes it to an extreme."

The statement of the article was, "The construction of the opinion that it is binding upon the other departments of the State and the citizens is one for which the opinion itself may not be alone responsible. That conclusion is derived from it in the able summary of the opinion in the editorial columns of the *Journal* It is considered, also, in other editorial columns, that the opinion is an insuperable barrier," etc. Again, "This opinion of the Court is not like a judgment, binding upon the parties before it, whether right or wrong. It is simply the opinion of the judges who signed it, carrying no force of obligation with it."

The reader in this instance, and throughout this reply, will decide to whom credit should be given for "the coinage of a too lively fancy," and by whom the alloy is added, in the reissue of the original statement.

The principal purpose of the paragraph seems to be to accuse the author of the article of having once, as counsel, claimed more weight for the opinion of the judges than he does now. According to the report of his argument in Taylor v. Place, as counsel in that case, he replied to the citation by opposite counsel from the opinion of the judges given to the Assembly as to the extent of its judicial powers, and said, it seems, that the part of the opinion cited by his opponent in favor of the power was an *obiter dictum*, something aside from the answer given to the inquiry of the Assembly. That direct answer he called *res judicata*.

It is the right and duty of an advocate in courts to present one side of a cause and the truths that make for his client and arguments that favor him, and to urge them strongly. It is the duty of a judge or a citizen giving his personal opinion to his fellow-citizens to state the balanced result, the final truth in his own mind.

The really important inquiry is, whether the position taken in the article as to the weight of an advisory opinion is a true one. To that the judgment in Taylor v. Place gives a decisive answer. To that answer the pamphlet does not refer. The ordinary reader of it is allowed to receive the impression that neither the court nor any judge had taken any position on this point.

What the Court does say is : "The advice or opinion given by the judges of this Court, when requested, to the governor, or to either house of the General Assembly, under the third section of the tenth article of the constitution, *is not a decision of this Court;* and given, as it must be, without the aid which the Court derives, in adversary cases, from able and experienced counsel, though it may afford much light from the reasonings or research displayed in it, *can have no weight as a precedent.*"

"The great Massachusetts chief justice," Shaw, and his colleagues have also said it "would be contrary to the plain dictates of justice, if such an opinion could be considered as having the force of a judgment, binding on the rights of parties."

The pamphlet proceeds : "Judge Bradley makes the point that the question on which the opinion was given is political, not judicial, and argues that it is for the General Assembly to decide it for the judges, rather than for the judges to decide it for the General Asembly. I do not care to contest the point with him ; but, conceding it, what follows?"

The article stated the position, and sustained it by quoting quite fully the opinion of the Supreme Court of Rhode Island, in the trial of T. W. Dorr, the adoption of that opinion by Mr. Webster in terms, and its adoption by the Supreme Court of the United States in the Rhode Island cases, and the corresponding decision in the Georgia case. The reader of the pamphlet has no intimation of this conclusive weight of authority in favor of the doctrine.

The chief justice, however, says, "It seems to me further that, as a matter of conscience — though I am no casuist — it will be better for them (the General Assembly) to follow it until they are clearly satisfied that it (the opinion) is wrong." In other words, the department of government, upon whose conscience and judgment the determination of such questions rests, is bound in conscience to follow the judgment of another department in the first instance, and only to disregard that opinion when "conclusively refuted," "whether the question be political or non-political." The pamphlet finally asks, "What is the use of befogging a plain matter by irrelevant distinctions?" It regards distinctions between opinions which, in the language of the Supreme Court in Taylor v. Place, "have no weight as a precedent," and those which are conclusive and also between judicial and political questions and departments as irrelevant.

The Supreme Court of this State, and of other States, and of the United States, does not so regard them, as the reader of the article and of this reply will perceive, though the reader of the pamphlet is not informed by it in this matter.

PERSONALITIES AND OTHER MATTERS INTRODUCED IN THE PAMPHLET.

The chief justice proceeds, and becomes still more personal. The assumption of the pamphlet gives full opportunity to retort these personal imputations. But they are unworthy of such a discussion.

The chief justice goes further, and says that "whenever he

(the author of the article) discovers a lack of weight in his argument he promptly throws his reputation, as a conqueror might throw his sword, into the ascending scale. A notable instance occurred last winter at a hearing before a committee of the General Assembly. Judge Bradley appeared before the committee, and, making a few remarks, handed to the members printed slips containing his argument. 'In answer to a question by Dr. Garvin,' says the Providence *Journal*, in its report of the hearing, 'Judge Bradley said that the constitution did not impliedly or explicitly prohibit the holding of a convention, but requires and confirms the right of the Assembly to initiate proceedings.' The reader will remark the absolute assurance of his answer. He puts his foot upon the opinion of five judges, as if it were simply an egg-shell, which he had only to step upon to crush it to atoms."

If any citizen is to attempt to refute an opinion, he must state the counter proposition; the first part of the sentence quoted was the counter proposition, the latter part was concurrent with the opinion. The former part was correctly reported. That is all that was said, and that in answer to a question, after having submitted the argument in print to the committee. Where is the assurance, in the exercise of this right or in such an attack upon a citizen because he expresses an opinion different from an advisory opinion of the judges?

It is not the weight of any man's foot, which, as he says, crushes the opinion like an egg-shell. It is the weight of historic fact and of the concurrent judgment of competent persons. The pamphlet will not prove any stronger though filled with what it ought not to contain.

The pamphlet, in a note, refers to some articles in the Providence *Journal*, and charges that they reflected upon the Court for not giving the reasons for its decisions upon questions of fact. The articles referred principally to the duty of giving reasons for decisions of questions of law. The neglect of this duty the pamphlet does neither deny nor defend. The pamphlet says the articles on "Proceedings in Court" contained many wise and valuable remarks. The attack and the commendation may justify their appearance in a supplement, with a continuation of them.

THE ACTS OF THE GENERAL ASSEMBLY IN 1853 PROVIDING FOR A CONSTITUTIONAL CONVENTION.

The chief justice next refers to a certain political action of the author of the pamphlet more than thirty years ago. The action was not individual, but concurrent with a majority of the General Assembly at that time. The action referred to is a part of the history of this question in this State. Its historic, not its personal aspect may have some interest for the reader.

Two acts submitted the question of holding a convention by those qualified to vote under the existing constitution, and provided that the delegates should be the same in numbers as the members of the Assembly from each town. In these respects it was like the provisions for the amendment to the constitution recently proposed by the adherents of the doctrine of the Court and rejected by the people.

The chief justice says that the " people, mindful of the lesson which they had learned in 1842," rejected the first act. Is he well advised in saying that? The principal opposition was in the columns of the *Post* in articles signed a "Democrat of '42." The writer was Thomas Wilson Dorr.

No argument against the constitutionality of the act, it is believed, was submitted in the Assembly, certainly not in the Senate ; and not in the *Journal* even. It contented itself with simple assertions until the second act, when an argument, not editorial, but contributed, appeared in its columns.

The act of October was not a simple act to revise the constitution, as it appears in the pamphlet. It was for limited purposes and specific changes only. The act submitted to the voters whether the delegates chosen in June, whose selection the *Journal* highly commended, should assemble to consider those questions only. Its terms were : "Shall the delegates elected on the 28th of June, A. D. 1853, under and by virtue of an act recommending a convention, passed at the last May session of the General Assembly, convene for the purpose of considering the expediency of framing a constitution of government of this State, different from the present constitution in these specific and only particulars, to wit, the abolition of the registry tax ; the extension of the time of registration as a qualification for voting ; and the districting the cities and larger towns of the State, in the election of representatives to the General Assembly ? "

The Democratic delegates from Smithfield, at the head of whom was Thomas Steere, then Speaker of the House, and for many years one of the editorial corps of the paper which has guided the public opinion of the State, and the delegates from North Providence, the youngest of whom was the present writer, issued addresses to the voters of their respective towns, pledging themselves to entertain no other proposition except those contained in the act. A majority of the members elected were also of the opposite party. This was the precise case contemplated in the second question and answer of the opinion of the Massachusetts judges, upon which the pamphlet and opinion rely.

The question and answer were as follows : —

" 2nd. Whether, if the Legislature should call a convention of delegates for the purpose of making a specific revision of the constitution in certain departments, that convention would have any power to go beyond those specific amendments proposed by the terms of the vote calling the convention?"

Ans. " If the Legislature should submit to the people the expediency of calling a convention to revise or alter the constitution in any specified part thereof, and the people should, by the terms of their vote, decide to call a convention, the delegates would derive their whole authority and commission *from such vote,* and would have no right, under the same, to propose amendments in other parts of the constitution not so specified."

The *Journal* had expressed its willingness that the registry tax should be abolished, but opposed the call of a convention ; and in its issue of Nov. 1, 1853, it said, " There will be no opposition to the repeal of the registry tax in the legal and constitutional mode." With the opposition of Thomas W. Dorr in the *Post* and this promise by Henry B. Anthony in the *Journal,* the project for the vital reform failed. The *Journal* concurred in the wisdom and expediency of such a change in the constitution. It promised that the change should be made by amendment. Its party has been in full power for thirty years, and the amendment has never been made.

The pamphlet says: "The payment (of the registry taxes) has long come to be regarded as a regular part of the election expenses, and certain high offices go almost as a matter of course to men who can make or secure large contributions to the necessary fund. And this, though bad enough, is not the worst, for the descent is easy from such a practice to downright bribery and corruption." The chief justice says: " While I condemn the tax, I cannot condemn the authors of it. They meant it for good, and they are not to blame, because, while they clearly saw the good which would result from its legitimate operation, they did not also foresee the evil to which it might be perverted." He is not historically just to some of the framers of the constitution. Elisha R. Potter said of "the system of voluntary taxation": "It was virtually setting up shops for the sale of the right of suffrage." Judge Potter was instructed in political knowledge not only by his own experience and education, but by his father, of whom tradition speaks as one of the greatest men in public life the State ever had. So Richard K. Randolph, whose high personal honor impressed all who met him, and illumined his judgment, says, on p. 52 of the journal of the convention, "that he was opposed to the report of the committee, and should vote for the amendment. He did so because he did not like the registry tax as a qualification. It was too much like selling the right of voting. It was saying to a man: The rights of electors are for sale, and you can enjoy them for a dollar a year. Besides, a great door was left open here for fraud. The tax might be paid by politicians, and thus induce a trade in votes."

After ten years of experience, these predictions had, to the minds of those who voted for the convention acts of 1853, proved true.

The pamphlet stands now — the *Journal* did then — in opposition to the only practical remedy for a most destructive evil.

There are those who profit by the continuance of this system; but one is not willing to expose the shame of the State, — the chief justice has spoken distinctly enough. Strong measures are justified, and experience shows they are demanded, for this system elevates the followers of Judas: they who give the bribes not less than they who take them betray the State.

When the acts of 1853 were passed, the horizon, both east and west, was full of light upon this constitutional question. Massachusetts had acted, New York had acted, other States also. Those States had held conventions to frame constitutions to be submitted to the people. Those conventions had assembled, pursuant to acts of legislation, and those acts of legislation had been passed under constitutions which contained provisions for amendment like our own, and did not contain any provision for calling conventions. We who had lived in this State had heard the question discussed; we had lived at a period when, as the pamphlet says, "men were led by the political upheaval of the time to study the entire volume, not only of political principles, but also of political practices." We knew that some men differed from us, but our own judgments and consciences were clear. Courts and legislatures and conventions and the general government itself have concurred in the opinion upon which we then acted. All was light then, and all is light now; there is but one cloud in the sky.

THE ACT OF THE ASSEMBLY IN REGARD TO T. W. DORR.

The chief justice mounts still higher in his scale of accusation, and says that the act of the General Assembly which revoked and annulled the judgment and sentence upon Thomas W. Dorr was an "unprecedented indignity" upon which he will not comment, and was a virtual adoption of the principles of Dorr, that a constitution might be changed with or without law. The grounds for that act are stated in its preamble. A copy of the preamble and the act will appear in the Appendix. The reasons of law and fact there stated have never met with any attempt at reply, except in an advisory opinion given to the General Assembly by the judges. What judgment was afterwards rendered by the Court upon that opinion fully appears in the decision in Taylor *v.* Place. The portion of that judgment relating to the opinion will also appear in the Appendix. That judgment not only condemns the major part of the opinion, but intimates very plainly that the part in which it concurs does not sustain that portion of the opinion that held the act to be unconstitutional.

Upon the question of the authority of the General Assembly to pass such an act, the chief justice will, of course, accept the opinion of his father, who was both a member of the convention that framed the constitution, and also chief justice of the State at the time. The elder Chief Justice Durfee opposed a motion to amend the provision in regard to the continuance of the previous powers of the General Assembly. The landholders' constitution was taken as the basis of the proceedings of the convention. In that constititution the provison was: "The General Assembly shall *continue to exercise the judicial power*, the power of visiting corporations, and all other powers they have heretofore exercised, not inconsistent with this constitution." When the phraseology of that provision was changed so as to read as it does in the present constitution does not appear. The description of powers retained is in effect the same ; the one specific, the other inclusive. It now reads, Article IV., Sect. 10 : "The General Assembly shall continue to exercise the powers they have heretofore exercised, unless prohibited in this constitution." A motion was made to amend it as follows (Journal of the Convention, page 65) : "Mr. Shearman offered a substitute for the eighteenth section of the fourth article. It took away from the General Assembly the appellate jurisdiction on petitions for divorce, benefit of the insolvent laws, new trials, and the jurisdiction on sales of real estate. After much debate, in which Messrs. Shearman and Potter advocated the amendment and Messrs. Simmons, Durfee, Nathan B. Sprague, and Updike opposed it, the amendment was rejected." So that the elder chief justice was opposed to any change of the provisions of the constitution which continued to the Assembly its revisory and appellate power over judicial proceedings. The last argument submitted by the pamphlet purports to be a portion of a charge given to the grand jury, in 1843, by the elder Chief Justice Durfee, and found among his papers. In that paper, as produced in the pamphlet, we find this statement : "With the exception of a few restrictions, the legislative power, by an express provision of the constitution, remains the same as under the charter." The elder Chief Justice Durfee was one of the committee to revise the statutes of the State, so that they should accord with the new constitution. Those statutes provided modes for taking appeals to the Assembly from the courts. The authority of the elder Chief Justice Durfee in favor of continuing the judicial power to the General Assembly, and his opinion that it was thus continued, are clear. This opinion was entertained by every one for years after the adoption of the constitution.

The power of the Assembly to pass such an act does not rest only upon its judicial power, as expressed in the charter and continued in the constitution. It is the power over judgments for treason always exercised by our English fathers in Parliament, not as a judicial power, and with the eminent approval of all later times. There are many cases. The act in one of these, Lord Russell's, is copied in the Appendix. Such power was exercised by the General Assembly the first year after the trial of Dorr in their act of amnesty and liberation, overturning the judgment of the court which condemned him to imprisonment for life at hard labor. That this power was not judicial and yet was constitutional, the Superior Court in Taylor v. Place well knew and recognized. They decided that the Assembly had not judicial power, and yet carefully avoided being understood to think that the reversal act was void.

"The judges gave their opinion that the act in question was unconstitutional and void, *as an exercise of judicial power prohibited by the constitution to the general assembly;* but not having that case now before us, for the purpose of ascertaining how far the prohibition in question *applied* to it." [Italicized by the Court] Besides, the indictment was found under the charter.

The pamphlet says (p. 54) : "There is an old maxim which in Latin reads, *Contemporanea expositio est optima,* and which in English means that contemporaneous construction is best. The reason for it is obvious. The men who make a law know what they mean by it, and therefore when, immediately after making it, they construe it by word or act, their construction is of high authority." The facts of this construction and of the origin of the constitution are stated in a paper written by the Hon. J. P. Knowles in 1858, and found in the Appendix.

The facts which the preamble to the act of the Assembly sets forth have not been controverted. One fact to the credit of the presiding justice, Chief Justice Durfee, should be known. He was strenuously opposed to the determination to put Dorr upon trial before the courts. This I know from a report of his conversation by my then partner, Charles F. Tillinghast, a name I never can permit myself to mention without an expression of respect.

The chief justice well knew that there had been a political controversy, going to the very verge of civil war, and ended by the application, through leading citizens of our State, to the general government for protection, which was granted. He fore-knew, also, that in the division which existed in the public mind, the endeavor to add to the political destruction of Dorr and his adherents, a conviction in the courts would prove a failure, or must be carried through with a strong hand, and in either event would be worse than useless. Other counsels prevailed, and the cause was tried, and what occurred appears in reports well-nigh forgotten, but still extant. The first Assembly elected after the trial of Dorr passed a general act of amnesty, and liberated him from imprisonment.

We print in the Appendix some extracts from the report of the trial.

They show, as does the report in the *Journal*, that the chief justice was strenuous that the members of one political party only should be put on the jury. They show that two of his colleagues, each of whom afterwards became chief justice, did not agree with him in his law. The Providence *Journal* did not. One hundred and seven out of one hundred and eight of the panel of the jury were from one party, and the jury itself was composed only of the members of that party.

If the author of the pamphlet chooses to wander from the question, and to assail, in the phrases he uses and in the accusations he makes, the majority of the General Assembly at that time, because they differ from him, without even reading the vindication of their act in its preamble, he must not complain if the facts of the trial as contained in a report of undoubted accuracy are brought out in response to the charge. It especially concerns that " one undeniable fundamental privilege " which Hallam says, " in the worst times except those of the late usurpation had been the standing record of primeval liberty, trial by jury." It touches other questions of moment somewhat aside from the present inquiry, and may be remanded to the Appendix.

HISTORIC ORIGIN OF THE QUESTION UNDER DISCUS-
SION. — ITS TERMS AS PROPOSED BY THE SENATE
TO THE JUDGES, AND THEIR ANSWER.

The chief justice passes by the historical argument of the
article, which is the main portion of it, and begins his "counter
argument" in a different order.

A brief statement of the facts out of which the question
arises is necessary to a fair understanding of what the question
is. There was originally but one, there are now two modes of
changing State constitutions, one by amendment by the Legisla
ture and people, the other by a change through a convention
elected for that special purpose, and acting under a law, and by
vote of the people. Sometimes one of these methods is provided in the constitution, sometimes both, sometimes neither.

The method by legislation never exists, except by express
provision; for a legislature elected to carry out a constitution
could not change it, except by special authority in the constitution so to do. Propositions are made by a legislature under
certain precautions as to time and modes, and the majority of it
required, lest the people might be surprised by sudden action.
Such a mode is convenient, also, in unimportant matters, or in
matters upon which there is no real difference of opinion among
the people, as in the four amendments made in our constitution.

The other method is the one in which the sovereign power over
constitutions is usually exercised in America. The sovereign in
such matters is the people. He who argues for that proposition,
Mr. Webster says, argues without an adversary. The people cannot act en masse upon such a subject: they must act by delegates
assembled in convention. Such is the usual American mode.
An unbroken current exists, says Mr. Webster, of law, of
precedent, and of practice, from the commencement of our
government down to the latest example at the date of his
argument (1845), that of New York. This method of change
has been pursued when the constitution contained provision for
legislative amendment, as our constitution does, just as uni-

formly as when it does not contain such provision. Instances of this first kind occur in such leading States as New York, Pennsylvania, Missouri, Georgia, Louisiana, Texas, Tennessee, Arkansas. The general government pursued the same course in the changes made by seceding and reconstructed States ; it required changes to be made by convention in States which had a provision for amendment in their constitution the same as in those States that did not. All this is fully shown in the article.

In the history of Rhode Island there have been a number of instances in which the General Assembly have exercised the power to call a constitutional convention. The General Assembly had, prior to the adoption of the present constitution, four times called conventions and invited the people to send their delegates to it ; and their laws provided that the action of the convention should be submitted to the vote of the people, and the result determined by a majority of votes. The two laws passed by the General Assembly since the adoption of the constitution left it to the legal voters by a majority vote to decide whether the convention should be held.

Our General Assembly, having this method of changing the State constitution in mind, submitted the following to the judges for their opinion : "A difference has arisen among members of the General Assembly as to the legal competency thereof, under the constitution of the State, to call upon the electors to elect members to constitute a convention to frame a new constitution of the State, and to provide that the new constitution should be submitted for adoption either to the qualified electors of the State or to the persons who would be entitled to vote under said new constitution for adoption, and if a majority of such electors, or persons voting, should vote in favor thereof, whether the new constitution would then become the legally adopted constitution of the State, and be binding, as such, upon all of the people thereof."

The second question was similar, on the supposition that the act of the Assembly should leave the question of calling a convention to the vote of the people.

The opinion answered the question in this wise : "We received from your Honors on the 24th inst. a resolution, requesting our opinion in regard to the legal competency of the General Assembly to call a convention for the revision of the Constitution. In reply, we have to say that we are of opinion that the mode provided in the Constitution for the amendment thereof is the only mode in which it can be constitutionally amended." It then gave the reasons for their opinion. A doubt has been expressed whether their opinion answered the entire question. The chief justice says (page 32) : "If the Assembly is shut up to the mode expressly provided, the people are also shut up to it, since the people cannot move in the matter of an amendment, without the initiative of the Assembly."

But he further says (page 48) : "But if a new constitution is established, resulting in the establishment of a new government, with the assent of the old, the change, though unconstitutional and revolutionary, is nevertheless effectual, and it cannot be reversed, within the State, without a counter revolution." It is therefore binding. The supposed case is of a change that is unconstitutional and revolutionary. The pamphlet appears to say that a change made by the sovereign power with the consent of the existing government would be revolutionary. "A revolution in politics is the consummation of a rebellion or revolt against the established or existing government."— *Worcester's Dictionary.* It is not properly applied to an act of the sovereign and existing government. The opinion does say that the act of the Assembly would be unconstitutional and void, so that the meaning of the judges is as interpreted and expressed by the chief justice, that though the act of the Assembly should be unconstitutional, still, if acted upon by the people and carried out, the new constitution would be binding.

The reasons given in the opinion were principally the rule of law *expressio unius,* which will be specially considered. Then a claim follows that the judges of the Supreme Court of Massachusetts have expressed a similar opinion. This claim has been and will be fully considered. Then after a description of the constitutional provision and the reasons for it, the inference is drawn that " it is inconceivable to us that they would have elaborated so guarded a mode of amendment, unless they had

ERRATUM.

On page 57, line 5, "twenty-eight" should read "over eight."
See further, pages 75, 76.

intended to have it exclusive and controlling." This inference
is met by the historic fact that such provisions have not been
so considered in about fifty State constitutions, which contained
the same provisions for amendment, and also provisions for a
convention, and by the fact that in twenty-eight instances conventions have been called where this provision for amendment
existed without any provision for a convention. The opinion
and pamphlet rest only upon an inference set up against the
usage of the country as to the meaning and effect of these provisions. Yet the pamphlet says (page 33) : "Certainly if any
instrument ought to be construed according to the common
usages of human speech, a constitution, adopted by the people
as the expression of their sovereign will, ought to be so construed, unless there is some reason, historic or other, for
construing it otherwise."

The opinion then proceeds to consider the question whether
the undertaking to frame a new constitution would be a different
one from making amendments to the existing constitution, and
says that the distinction " is, in their opinion, rather specious
than sound." In this, again, they stand alone as against the historic recognition of the difference and distinction. The opinion
assumes that nothing but a "superstructure and details" will
have to be considered. *The Federalist* said the definition of
the right of suffrage is very justly regarded as a fundamental
article of republican government. Questions of suffrage and
the apportionment of political power are those considered in the
pamphlet. They are fundamental. The Legislature, the chief
justice says, "is not generally well fitted to decide legal or
constitutional questions." Shall it exclude the usual American
method, — a convention by delegates specially selected for this
purpose, whose members are not necessarily from the vicin-
age which selects them, but chosen at the option of the towns
throughout the State ?

And again, is it best that such questions should be decided
by a minority instead of by a majority of the people? The latter is the American and the European method when any constitutional matter is submitted to popular vote. There is only one
solitary exception to this besides Rhode Island. This inquiry

will be further considered. The opinion concludes that there are no rights to be considered except those derived from a written constitution. In all these matters the pamphlet follows the opinion. The opinion follows, in turn, the report of a committee of the Assembly of 1882. A portion of that report, which anticipates the principal portions of the opinion and the pamphlet, appears in the Appendix, marked "Z." The pamphlet, as a most carefully prepared and elaborated statement, will receive a full reply, with an endeavor, however, to disregard its studied offensiveness of expression.

THE PAMPHLET ASSUMES THAT THE POSITION IN THE ARTICLE IS THAT THERE CANNOT BE AN IMPLIED PROHIBITION OF THE POWER IN QUESTION. THE ARTICLE DENIES THAT THE RULE RELIED UPON BY THE OPINION WORKS SUCH PROHIBITION. QUOTATIONS FROM PAMPHLET AND ARTICLE.

The pamphlet in opening the discussion says : "The judges, in their opinion, yielding to this declaration, maintained that the constitution having provided a mode for its own amendment, the enactment of any different mode by the General Assembly would be void. The correctness of this proposition seems, at first blush, too plain for controversy. Its opponents attempt to controvert it in this way: The constitution, they argue, though it provides a particular mode of amendment, does not prohibit amendment in other modes, and, therefore, an amendment through the medium of a constitutional convention, without following the provision, is valid. The argument, it will be observed, rests on the assumption that the power cannot be deemed to have been prohibited to the General Assembly, because it is not prohibited by words of express negation." The reader may compare the statement of the question and of the opinion with the terms of each previously quoted.

The position of the opponents of the opinion of the judges is not correctly or truly stated in the pamphlet. "Their argument" does not " rest on the assumption that the power" (to provide for a convention by legislation) " cannot be deemed to have been prohibited to the General Assembly because it is not prohibited by words of express negation." A full comparison of the statement of the positions of the article as made in the pamphlet, with the statements of the article itself, will now be made. In one place the pamphlet says : "The assertion that the sovereign power of the people cannot be limited by implication has so imposing a sound that the unwary reader might easily be led to accept it as a legal aphorism ; but, nevertheless, I venture to deny it, and to call for authority in support of it."

Again (page 35), and in more offensive terms, it says, of the seceding States : " That in one matter, they took the same position that Judge Bradley took. They maintained that the States, though they had united to form the Union, had never expressly agreed that the Union should be indissoluble, and that their power could not be limited by implication. This doctrine was confuted on the battle-fields, and disaffirmed by the courts," etc., " and ought to be regarded as too thoroughly discredited to find a place anywhere out of the limbo of exploded errors."

Again, it is said (page 45) : " The idea that the exercise of the power can be prohibited only by express negation, is utterly untenable. For if it were tenable, mark the result : The General Assembly, under the old charter, was accustomed to exercise power over the right of suffrage, restricting or extending it. It is nowhere prohibited, by express negation, from continuing to exercise the power ; but, certainly, no one, not a fanatic nor a fool, will have the effrontery to maintain that it can still continue to exercise it. There is a kind of reasoning which the logicians call a *reductio ad absurdum*, which consists in showing that a proposition must be erroneous because it is absurd. It seems clear to my mind that the proposition which I am combating is of that character."

Now let us see the position of the article in regard to an implied prohibition, and what is the ground upon which it opposes the rule relied upon by the court. The article stated, early in the discussion, "as to Mr. Webster's opinion, that the people may in their constitutions put restrictions upon their own actions, that is not the question now in issue. The present question is whether the American provisions for legislative amendment of a constitution is a prohibition of their power to change a constitution through the medium of a convention, and by a vote of the people, acting under the sanction and safeguards of an ordinary act of legislation which calls for a convention and provides for its action."

Again, toward the conclusion, in considering the question of an implied prohibition, the article reads : "It is said that there can be an implied prohibition. Taylor v. Place is cited for this doctrine. The principle there acted upon is thus stated : 'Affirmative words, vesting power under a constitution, are construed as prohibiting the exercise of the power by all other departments of the government, tribunals or officers, as the case may be, when, otherwise, the words would have no operation at all, or not their full and proper operation.' In Marbury v. Madison, the case referred to in this case, Marshall, C. J., said : 'A negative or exclusive sense must be given to them or they have no operation at all.' It certainly cannot be claimed that the amendatory power given to the General Assembly cannot operate or exist while the reforming power over their constitution by the people, through a convention and act of the Assembly, also exists. The coexistence of these powers have been manifested in terms and in action under nearly fifty State constitutions in this country."

The article, it will be observed, stated the doctrine on which these cases rest in the language of the courts, and then pointed out that the doctrine did not apply to the present question. Neither did the opinion of the judges nor the pamphlet claim that it does. The opinion cited Taylor v. Place to show, "That an implied is as effectual as an expressed prohibition." And the pamphlet does not controvert the correctness of the statement of the doctrine nor the soundness of the conclusion, that the doctrine does not apply to the present question ; it says, as before, simply : "In Taylor v. Place, 4 R. I. 324, the Supreme Court decided that an implied is as effectual as an express prohibition." That proposition has not been denied.

The pamphlet, however, without quoting any portion of what the article did contain, attempts a reply. It assumes that it contains the idea of which the pamphlet accuses its opponents; that there may be an expressed and cannot be an implied prohibition. Its reply is in these terms : "Judge Bradley attempts to limit the authority of Taylor v. Place, but the attempt, contrary to his wont, is rather blind, and it certainly is not successful"; and then adds what has once been quoted about a fanatic and a fool — once is enough. This is the way in which the pamphlet states the position of an opponent and the way it meets it.

The position that was taken in the article in regard to the rule is shown in the conclusion of its argument : —

"There are three provisions of our constitution by which these rights are secured to the people in the Assembly. First, the general grant of legislative power which we have seen includes this power ; second, the express reservation of the entire right of the whole proceeding in the first section of that Bill of Rights which is declared to be of paramount obligation upon all departments of the government ; and third, the express provision that 'The General Assembly shall continue to exercise the powers they have heretofore exercised unless prohibited in this constitution.'

"There can be no implied prohibition under the rule relied upon in the opinion and report, because the rule only applies by its very terms to methods and powers not expressed. The Latin expressions of the rule, in words that have been so anglicized as to be intelligible to all, express the rule with brevity and clearness : —

"*Expressio unius exclusio est alterius. Expressum facit cessare tacitum.*

"The expression of one method is the exclusion of the alternative method not expressed. The express causes the tacit (unexpressed) to cease.

"The whole argument for prohibition in our constitution rests upon the assumption that the power is nowhere expressed or reserved. This assumption is manifestly unfounded."

This is the statement of the principal objection to the application of the rule relied upon by the judges. To the correctness of the version of the rule as thus stated no exception is taken in the pamphlet. The law is not guilty of such absurdity as to say that of two powers conferred in an instrument, one excludes the other, nor does it say that a power specifically expressed is to exclude another which is described in general terms.

But the pamphlet, while not controverting the meaning of the rule, still relies, as did the opinion, upon the rule of law, *Expressio unius exclusio est alterius*, for the conclusion which was stated to the Assembly. It says : —

"Now the judges, applying this principle, held that, a particular mode of amendment being presented, any other mode was prohibited by implication, although no prohibitory language was employed. . . . The old Roman jurists saw this centuries ago, as clearly as we see it to-day, and accordingly laid down the rule, '*expressio unius est exclusio alterius*,' which is as much a rule of our law as of theirs. The judges, in their opinion, apply this rule to the constitution for the purpose of getting at its meaning."

The idea of the pamphlet, it may be remarked in passing, as to what is the ground of an implication of prohibition from affirmative words is peculiar. It takes, as an illustration, the article in the Bill of Rights, that the right of trial by jury shall remain inviolate, as if the expression was not in terms a prohibition, — as if it was not the precise equivalent of saying that the right should not be violated by any department of the government. The pamphlet says, "It only declares that the right of trial by jury shall remain inviolate, and from this affirmative language the prohibition is implied. Other examples might be given."

THE ARGUMENT OF THE PAMPHLET BEGINS WITH A CHARACTERISTIC PREFACE.

The position of the article and of the pamphlet having been thus ascertained, we now proceed to consider what the pamphlet submits by way of argument. It says : "Now let us consider the reasons which Judge Bradley opposes to this construction. His first reason is that the rule applied by the judges, however applicable it may be in private matters, is not applicable to limit the sovereign power ; or, in other words, that the power of the people, including their power to amend their form of government, cannot be limited by implication." Here again is the substitution of one thing for another. To say that a certain rule is not applicable so as to be the ground for an implied prohibition, is a very different thing from the assertion that the power of the people, including the power to amend their form of government, cannot be limited by implication. Rather oddly the pamphlet observes in the next sentence: "The wide-awake reader will here detect a specimen of the logical legerdemain which is sometimes resorted to by the skilful advocate." The writer did not intend to apply this sentence to his own performance, but to apply it to his opponent. And he adds, "The judges maintained that the constitution having provided one mode of amendment, the General Assembly could not provide another, their power being limited by implication. Judge Bradley, adroitly substituting the people for the Assembly, replies that the power of the people cannot be limited by implication. Why does he make the substitution? He makes it because he knows that the power of the Assembly can be limited by implication, and is so limited in our constitution. He has some excuse, however; for if the Assembly is shut up to the mode expressly provided, the people are also shut up to it, since the people cannot move in the matter of an amendment without the initiatives of the Assembly. But though this may be some excuse for the substitution, it does not justify it."

The degree of truth and courtesy characteristic of the pamphlet appears in this quotation from it. What the judges did say was: "That the mode provided in the constitution for the amendment thereof, is the only mode in which it can be constitutionally amended." The pamphlet substitutes for this the statement: "The constitution having provided one mode of amendment, the General Assembly could not provide another."

The article said: "The rule does not apply to provisions in statutes so as to take away any right of the sovereign power." The phrase, "any right of the sovereign power," was adopted as equivalent to the phrase, "rights of the Crown," used by Dwarris, an English writer, and quoted in the next sentence of the article.

The pamphlet says that Judge Bradley, "adroitly substituting the people for the Assembly," replies "that the power of the people cannot be limited by implication." No such change was made. Neither word was used. It could not have been made, as there was no opportunity for it in the language already used in the opinion. Such change would have been useless also, for the pamphlet admits that whether the people or the Assembly are the words used, the result, as far as this question is concerned, would be the same. The motive charged for the alleged substitution was an insult that is not entitled to an answer. A writer who has made three substitutions in a single breath, as it were, is in such an atmosphere that everything appears to him to be an adroit substitution from motives of deception.

The pamphlet says (page 34) : "The assertion that the sovereign power of the people cannot be limited by implication, has so imposing a sound that the unwary reader might easily be led to accept it as a legal aphorism ; but, nevertheless, I venture to deny it, and to call for authority in support of it."

"Judge Bradley has adduced what he claims to be authority. Let us examine it. In the first place, he adduces a rule laid down in Dwarris on Statutes, that the rights of the crown can never be taken away by doubtful words or ambiguous expressions, but only by *express terms.*"

The article said (and comment is unnecessary) : —

"We leave the historic view of the subject and proceed to briefly consider the legal reasoning upon which the opinion and report rest. The rule of law relied upon is stated to be that 'where power is given to do a thing in a particular way, then the affirmative words marking out the particular way prohibit all others by implication, so that the particular way is the only way in which the power can be legally exercised.' The Court further say : 'We do not see why it (the rule) is not as trustworthy a guide to the meaning, when the language so used occurs in a State constitution, as when it occurs in a statute or a will.'

"This rule does not apply to provisions in a statute so as to take away any right of the sovereign power.

"The rights of the crown can never be taken away by doubtful words or ambiguous expressions, but only by express terms." — Dwarris on Statutes, 706.

THE PAMPHLET, DIFFERING FROM THE OPINION, STATES THAT THE POWER IN THE ASSEMBLY TO PROVIDE FOR A CONSTITUTIONAL CONVENTION IS INCLUDED IN THE GENERAL GRANT OF LEGISLATIVE POWER. ITS PROHIBITION THEN CANNOT BE IMPLIED UNDER THE RULE RELIED UPON IN THE OPINION AND PAMPHLET.

The writer will now call attention to some of the propositions in which the article and the pamphlet agree. The article had said that a power expressed in the constitution could not be prohibited by the provision for amendment under the rule relied upon by the judges. This position has not been controverted by the chief justice, nor can it, indeed, be controverted by any one. The meaning of the rule is known to every boy in the profession, and is obvious to every man of sense. As has been said, the law is not guilty of the absurdity of saying that of two expressed modes, one excludes the other; nor does it say that the specific expression of one excludes the other when described in general terms.

Another doctrine upon which an agreement exists is thus stated in the article: "That the power to pass an act providing for a convention of the people of a State to reconstruct their State constitution exists in the legislature of a State, unless it has been prohibited, no one will dispute. It need not be specifically granted. It exists by force of this creation, or in the grant to one branch of the government of general legislative power. The Legislature of our State has that power, unless prohibited, as a part of its prerogative and right; not *ex-necessitate*, as the opinion says." Upon this point the pamphlet says: "The real fact is this, that the General Assembly has no power except that which the people, which it represents, have conferred upon it, either expressly or implicitly, in the constitution. Judge Bradley virtually admits this latter in his argument. The judges, in their opinion, had said that, in the absence of any express provision, the General Assembly would have the power to initiate constitutional change, *ex-necessitate* by implication and without restriction. Judge Bradley, correcting this, declares that the power is legislative power included in the general grant. Doubtless this is the better view."

The chief justice thus asserts a different doctrine from that of the opinion of the judges as to the ground upon which the Assembly formerly did or might exercise the power in question. They say it was an implied power from necessity, and he says that it is a part of the ordinary legislative power. "By this change," to use his own phrase, "he undermines his own argument."

HISTORIC FACTS AND PRINCIPLES OF AMERICAN CONSTITUTIONAL STATE GOVERNMENTS.

Now let us proceed to look at the subject from a more comprehensive point of view, not omitting, however, to consider fully every suggestion of the pamphlet. In the first place, the historic fact lies outstretched before us of a century of American constitutional existence. Throughout that period constitutions almost as numerous as the years have been changed by legislation, convention, and a majority vote of the people. This is the one great fact of American constitutional law known to all. Now, what are the principles of these State governments?

First. That the people of each State are sovereign, restrained only by the constitution of the United States. Mr. Webster says: "Well, then, let all admit, what none deny, that the only source of political power in this country is the people. Let us admit that they are *sovereign*, for they are so; that is to say, the aggregate community, the collected will of the people, is sovereign." (Webster's Works, Vol. VI. p. 222.)

Second. That this sovereignty is expressed by the majority of the people, and not by a minority. Mr. Webster again says, "He knew no principle that could prevent a majority, even a bare majority, of the people from altering the constitution." (Proceedings Massachusetts Convention, 1820, page 407.) Mr. Curtis says: "The American constitutions, therefore, are founded wholly upon the principle that a majority expresses the will of the whole society, and may establish, change and abrogate forms of government at its pleasure."* Such has been the practice of all the States, with one exception. Jameson says, p. 498 : "On the popular vote to ratify the action of the legislature a majority was required in all cases but that of Rhode Island (1842), which made a vote of three fifths of the people necessary."

Third. As the people, or a majority, cannot act *en masse*, they assemble, as the phrase is, in conventions, through delegates whom they appoint by their suffrages to represent them. All the constitutions that have existed and that now exist have been framed by such conventions, and submitted to the vote of the people.

Fourth. Experience taught that some less elaborate mode of amendment of a constitution might be expedient for minor changes or changes on which all were agreed. And powers were introduced, after the lapse of a generation, into some State constitutions, allowing the Legislature to propose such changes to the people to be determined by their majority vote. This was not a part of the legislative power. It required a special authority in the constitution. As Mr. Webster said, "This was not an exercise of legislative power : it was only referring to some branch the power of making propositions to the people." (Proceedings of Massachusetts Convention, 1820, page 407.)

Fifth. This method of legislative proposal has not superseded the convention method in a single State. They are recognized as coexistent methods of change in nearly fifty constitutions. The convention method has been pursued when the amendment method was provided, and there was no provision in terms for a convention, in the leading States of the Union.

Sixth. To claim, in Rhode Island, that the provision for legislative amendment takes the place of the convention, is to violate a fundamental principle of American State governments, — that a majority, not a minority, determines the question of

---

* In Vol. I of Curtis's History of Constitutional Law, p. 262.

change. That provision in the present constitution of Rhode Island requires more than a majority (three fifths) of the popular vote to adopt an amendment. No provision requiring more than a majority of the popular vote to adopt an amendment exists in any of the many constitutions that have existed, or now exist, containing provisions for legislative amendment. And of nearly one hundred constitutions which now exist, or have existed in this country, there is but one — that of New Hampshire of 1792 — which requires more than a majority to adopt a constitution proposed by a convention.

The following may interest the reader: A learned friend, whose name, did his modesty permit me to give it, would be entirely trustworthy, sends me a note in regard to the modes of changing the constitutions of the cantons of the Republic of Switzerland. Each cantonal constitution prescribes the method of partial or total revision of the constitution. Ordinarily this may be brought on as well by the people as by the authorities. In the former case (that of popular initiative) it is commonly required that a certain portion of the citizens should demand a submission of the question whether a revision shall be undertaken, to the people. If the submission is made, it is usual to couple with it the question whether the people will submit the revision to the Grand Council (i. e., the ordinary legislative body) or to a constituent assembly (i. e., an assembly chosen for the purpose of considering changes in the constitution). When the revision is total, the second method is preferred; when simply partial, the first is preferred. The result of their deliberations is submitted to the people and determined by a majority vote. If it is accepted by the people, it then needs the federal guarantee.

Our pamphlet has a different idea, and different knowledge from any one else on the subject. It says (page 54): "Is it not clear, then, that his meaning is that the people secure their forms of government from hasty changes by simple majorities by prescribing modes of amendment which require the consent of more than simple majorities? That is evidently what he means. He mentions no other way, and, so far as I know, there was no other way in which such security was made in any State constitution."

The author, failing thus in historic knowledge, is unable to perceive and to reason from the great fact and the experience of the century. He says (page 36) : To look upon anything outside of the written constitution is to look upon a " hypothetical nebula." To found an argument on the existence of the usage and practice of the country in changing their constitutions is a " most egregious fallacy."

When our constitution says this General Assembly shall continue to exercise the powers it has heretofore exercised, it calls upon us to look into past history. When it says in the last section of the Bill of Rights, " The enumeration of the foregoing rights shall not be construed to impair or deny others retained by the people," it means that the parchment is not the only thing at which the people may look. When the elder Chief Justice Durfee, in the memorandum quoted in the pamphlet, spoke of " fundamental principles of individual rights which lie at the foundation of all constitutional governments," he had some meaning. When Webster spoke of this uniform current, from the very commencement of our government of law, of precedent, and of practice in the mode of changing constitutions, he stated a fact of the weightiest moment. Such a fact may well be termed a part of the common law of our government, as jurists and statesmen have been accustomed to do ; see the quotations from the courts in Pennsylvania, and Senator, afterwards Vice-President Wilson, in this reply. The Supreme Court of New Hampshire, in an opinion in the 3d vol. p. 534 of their reports, illustrates the capacity to look outside of the words of a constitution. They say : " But the power of the Legislature to take the property of individuals for public purposes is indisputable. It is a power limited, undoubtedly, in its nature by the public exigencies ; but it is a power recognized by the constitution. There is no doubt, that when this power is exercised, a just compensation is to be made. The constitutions of some of the States expressly declare, that such compensation shall be made, and natural justice speaks on this point, where our constitution is silent." Webster and Mason, perhaps, never excelled at the bar of America, founded their argument in the Dartmouth College case on the same doctrine.

THREE CLAUSES IN THE CONSTITUTION WHICH GIVE THE POWER TO PASS AN ACT PROVIDING FOR A CONSTITUTIONAL CONVENTION; ALSO, THE PROVISION OF THE CONSTITUTION GIVING THE GENERAL ASSEMBLY POWER TO PROPOSE AMENDMENTS.

There are two other provisions, three in all, in the constitution, which confer the power of calling for conventions, and through the action of Legislature, convention, and popular vote, revising the constitution.

That each of these provisions, standing by itself, confers this power, the pamphlet admits. But its admission is not necessary to establish the construction of these clauses. For these three reasons, therefore, the rule relied upon in the opinion and the pamphlet does not apply.

These three powers are, in terms, as follows: —

"ARTICLE I.

"DECLARATION OF CERTAIN CONSTITUTIONAL RIGHTS AND PRINCIPLES.

"In order effectually to secure the religious and political freedom established by our venerated ancestors, and to preserve the same for our posterity, we do declare that the essential and unquestionable rights and principles hereinafter mentioned, shall be established, maintained, and preserved, and shall be of paramount obligation in all legislative, judicial, and executive proceedings."

"SECT. 1. In the words of the Father of his Country, we declare that 'the basis of our political systems is the right of the people to make and alter their constitutions of government'; but that the constitution which at any time exists, till changed by an explicit and authentic act of the whole people, is sacredly obligatory upon all."

This is in accordance with the American Constitutional Law, as shown by history, and is but the recognition and enactment of previously existing rights.

"OF THE LEGISLATIVE POWER.

" SECT. 1. This constitution shall be the supreme law of the State, and any law inconsistent therewith shall be void. The General Assembly shall pass all laws necessary to carry this constitution into effect."

" SECT. 10. The General Assembly shall continue to exercise the powers they have heretofore exercised, unless prohibited in this constitution."

The provision conferring upon the Legislature the power to propose amendments and prescribing the mode in which it should be exercised is as follows : " The General Assembly may propose amendments to this constitution by the votes of a majority of all the members elected to each house. Such propositions for amendment shall be published in the newspapers, and printed copies of them shall be sent by the Secretary of State, with the names of all the members who shall have voted thereon, with the yeas and nays, to all the town and city clerks in the State. The said propositions shall be, by said clerks, inserted in the warrants or notices by them issued, for warning the next annual town and ward meetings in April ; and the clerks shall read said propositions to the electors when thus assembled, with the names of all the representatives and senators who shall have voted thereon, with the yeas and nays, before the election of senators and representatives shall be had. If a majority of all the members elected to each house at said annual meeting shall approve any proposition thus made, the same shall be published and submitted to the electors in the mode provided in the Act of Approval ; and if then approved by three fifths of the electors of the State present, and voting thereon in town and ward meetings, it shall become a part of the constitution of the State."

THE MEANING OF THE WORDS "MAY" AND "SHALL" IN THE PROVISION FOR AMENDMENT CONSIDERED.

The pamphlet calls attention to the distinction between the grant of the power and the direction as to the mode of its exercise. The writer thinks that the opinion of the Court did not lay sufficient stress on this distinction. He says: "I come now to a point which I think did not receive the prominence it is entitled to in the opinion of the judges." The pamphlet says: "It [the provision] begins by giving the General Assembly leave to propose amendments. The language is purely permissive. The Assembly may or may not propose as it chooses." In directing "the steps which are to be taken there is an entire change in the form of expression. The language ceases to be permissive, and becomes peremptory. It is not 'may,' but 'shall,' 'shall,' 'shall.'" The pamphlet thinks this phraseology is so conclusive a denial of the power to call a convention that it says: "I will not multiply words. The demonstration is complete without them."

The purely permissive language of the constitution, in conferring the power to propose amendments, is conclusive that it was not binding upon the Legislature to act under it. It does not say that amendments shall or must be made through proposals from the General Assembly, or that the General Assembly shall make proposals (as in their judgment expedient) for amendments of the constitution. There are none of the words of command usual in constitutions when a duty is imposed. A mere permission to them to act is certainly not in terms exclusive of the modes of revision known and used for over sixty years throughout the country, and four times adopted in Rhode Island.

The provisions as to the mode of the exercise of the power are directory and mandatory. How the power if resorted to by the Assembly is to be carried into execution must be provided. No general law and custom existed for such a proceeding. It was a novel power conferred upon the General Assembly, and the mode of its exercise, wherever it has been conferred, has been pointed out. There is in those words no evidence of an intent to exclude the operation of the other power. A mere permission is not exclusive.

THE POWER TO CALL A CONSTITUTIONAL CONVENTION NOT LIMITED BY THE TERMS OF THE PROVISION FOR LEGISLATIVE AMENDMENT.

We have seen attempts at the substitution of expressions of the pamphlet in place of those of the article in stating its position. We now come to an attempt to state such position by quotation. And even in this the pamphlet is stating a meaning different from the article. And this is accomplished by taking a single sentence apart from its context. The position taken in this reply is also in the article; in discussing the applicability of the rule, *expressio unius*, etc., it said, "there is, therefore, no room for any implied prohibition, for there is an express grant of the power in question by a general grant of legislative powers which includes it." The next sentence was, "The rule does not apply for the further reason." Yet the pamphlet quotes the first sentence as a denial of any possible limitation upon a granted power.

Assume that a general grant may have limitations. The question remains, Is the grant in the general power thus limited by the provision for amendment? The pamphlet says, on page 36 : "The literary plan of the constitution requires that the grant of power, as included in the general grant, shall be expressed in one place, and the mode of exercising it prescribed in another." The power that is included in the general grant is confessedly the power to pass an act pursuant to which a convention to frame a constitution may be elected, and the constitution submitted to the vote of the people. In other words, that the mode of proceeding universally adopted in this country for a century in making a new constitution may be adopted. The provision for self-amendment in the constitution, by which the Legislature submits the proposed amendment to the people, confers a power upon the Legislature; that power is not contained in the general grant of legislative power or by that common law of our government, as the Pennsylvania court termed it, and which Webster described as the current of law of precedent and of practice. It exists only by force of a special provision in a constitution; it is contained in some and not in others.

The pamphlet says that the first power is included in the general clause, which is true. It then says that the mode of exercising is prescribed in another provision; it certainly is not in terms; no such provision was necessary, the mode was simple and well known. The pamphlet points out the provision which it claims prescribes the mode of exercising that power. The provision grants the power to amend by proposals from the Legislature only, and points out the mode of the exercise of such power under such a grant, and the mode of its exercise is necessarily a matter of special provision in a constitution. This is apparent from the nature of the power and from the historic fact concerning it.

To say that the mode of exercising the greater and inherent power is prescribed in the provision conceding and providing a method for the exercise of the lesser power, which depends on such provision for its existence, is an obvious error.

CHANGES BY LEGISLATIVE AMENDMENT AND THROUGH CONVENTION PRACTICALLY DIFFERENT.

The pamphlet next proceeds to claim that provisions for amendment in a State constitution are not different from provisions for a change of constitution by legislation, convention, and vote of the people. There is certainly reason for greater caution and more time in regard to changes, which may be proposed by an accidental majority in the Legislature before they are allowed to ripen into a permanent part of the constitution, because the public mind of the State may not have been called to a consideration of the change or had an opportunity to pass upon it; whereas, in the case of the convention, the attention of the State is called to the fact that the convention is assembled for the very purpose of making constitutional changes. There is an election of delegates for that special purpose, and as in the latter instance in our own State, they were called to vote upon the question whether there should be a convention.

In the nature of things, there may be often, as there has been four times in our own State, occasion for some slight changes in the constitution which can be conveniently adopted through legislation and vote of the people. Upon some important changes there may be a general consent. On the other hand, large and doubtful changes may be proposed, which should be canvassed by the best wisdom of the State, composed of delegates chosen without restriction of locality, and assembled in convention, and their work afterwards submitted to the people. That these two classes of changes exist from time to time is obvious in the nature of things. Practical wisdom in forming constitutions should make provision for either method. Instances of both methods are found to have been exercised in the history of the States of this Union times without number. In more constitutions which have been from time to time adopted than there are States in this Union, the two methods have existed side by side.

The historical argument, that drawn from the facts of American history, showing the concurring judgment and action of many and leading States in the Union, is briefly passed over. The facts are not stated in the pamphlet. The article points out the States which have changed their constitutions, and the dates when such changes occurred, and the provisions of previous constitutions concerning amendments and changes. The cases in which changes have been made under constitutions containing similar provisions to that of Rhode Island, with no provision for calling a convention, are New York (1845), Missouri (1865, convention called also in 1845), Louisiana (1852, 1864), Mississippi (1868), Tennessee (1870), Pennsylvania (1873), Arkansas (1874), Texas (1875). In Massachusetts a convention was called in 1853. Besides these instances the following States which had provisions like our own were restored, pursuant to acts of Congress, by means of conventions, and not by legislative action: Alabama, Arkansas, Georgia, Louisiana, Mississippi, Tennessee, and Texas. The pamphlet replies to these facts, that many of the States were seceding States, and the author of the pamphlet does not think much of their precedents. The pamphlet frequently indulges in such reflections upon these States. Grievously have those States erred, and grievously have they answered it. Those whose homes the war did not touch should not use its sad memories for unnatural purposes.

With the facts of the century before him, the pamphlet says, with great simplicity (page 41): "But why a convention is necessary, or what is the nature of that virtue which it can impart, he does not tell us; and I confess I cannot conjecture." It is simply the American mode of considering proposed organic changes; tumultuous popular meetings cannot do it; legislatures not well, if the opinion of the pamphlet is correct.

He further says: —

"It rests on the idea that a convention gets from the legislature or from the people, or from the legislature and the people, in some mysterious way, a power which neither the legislature nor the people, nor the legislature and the people both together have without it. Such a doctrine savors of miracle or necromancy, and it is at any rate too transcendental for me; for whatever other merit it may have, it lacks the sovereign merit of common-sense." Such ideas the pamphlet sets up and then assails them with such words.

Let us turn from that kind of discourse to the author who has made a special study of the subject of conventions. Mr. Jameson says of the American method of revising the fundamental law: —

"The legislature, forbidden itself to meddle with it, calls a convention to revise the fundamental law. The convention matures a scheme of amendments which it deems necessary, and recommends them, but ventures to conclude nothing. The electors, the ultimate body of functionaries, take up the *projet* which the convention has forged into shape, and temper and vitalize it by a power derived from the sovereign itself, and which they wield as its immediate representatives. Such is the distribution of functions exhibited in the work of fundamental legislation." (Jameson, 457.)

And of the mode of amendment by legislative propositions, he further says : —

"It ought to be confined, in my judgment, to changes which are simple or formal, and, therefore, of comparatively small importance. For a general revision of a constitution, or even for single propositions involving radical changes as to the policy of which the popular mind has not been informed by prior discussion, the employment of this mode is impracticable or of doubtful expediency." (Jameson, 495.)

One concession at the close may be noted. The writer says : "When I say this, however, I do not mean to say that the General Assembly cannot call a convention to prepare amendments, or even to prepare them in the form of a new constitution, but I mean to say this only" ; but in substance, that the people and convention are powerless to act, except through the methods pointed out in the constitution for amendments proposed by a legislature only. There is another recognition of the right under the constitution of the Assembly to call a convention to prepare a new constitution.

The admission of the chief justice that it is the right of the Assembly to call a convention, either to prepare amendments or a new constitution, leaves the question in this position : shall a constitution thus formed be submitted to the people as has been the practice of probably nearly a hundred instances in this country? In some rare case the action of the convention may have been final. Shall it afterwards be subjected to the novel device in such cases proposed by the chief justice, and to all the provisions to which the States have wisely subjected the powers of amendment by the legislature? It would seem that there should be some reason offered for such a novel view beyond the mere assertion of the chief justice "that I mean to say this only."

The chief justice had said (page 46) : "I desire to speak respectfully and without offence ; but, nevertheless, I must say that, in my opinion, a legislature is not generally well fitted to decide legal or constitutional questions."

To subject an amendment or a new constitution, framed by

the people in convention assembled, by delegates chosen for
that purpose, to the action of two successive legislatures, of
whom the chief justice has just given us his opinion, and,
further, to require that the result of the labors of such convention should not be accepted by a majority vote of the people,
but in disregard of the universal method of adoption by majorities, a fundamental idea of American government should be accepted only by a vote of three fifths of the people, is certainly
a novel device in constitutional law.

THE PROVISION IN THE BILL OF RIGHTS.

The pamphlet proceeds to consider the declaration of the
Bill of Rights, Sect. 1, Art. I.:   In the words of the Father
of his Country, we declare, that "the basis of our political
systems is the right of the people to make and alter their
constitutions of government; but that the constitution which at
any time exists, till changed by an explicit and authentic act of
the whole people, is sacredly obligatory upon all." The first
inquiry is, what do these words mean? Does "an explicit and
authentic act of the whole people" include the proceeding by
legislature, convention, and the people, by which constitutions
have always been changed? The article had said: "No one
will have the hardihood to deny that the act by which, throughout more than a century, the constitutions of the States of this
Union have been made and unmade, is an explicit and authentic
act for that purpose. None will so insult the character of
Washington as to assume that in the use of that phrase in his
Farewell Address he did not refer to that mode of change which
he had so often witnessed around him, the only methods known
at that time."

The chief justice says: "I agree that it means this in its
retrospective application, for our fathers proceeded in that
manner when they adopted our present constitution." But he
says its meaning was changed after the constitution was
adopted. Constitutions are made to operate in the future, not
in the past. The question rife in Rhode Island was, whether the

changes desired by a majority of its people could be made by a constitution adopted by convention assembled without the sanction of law, and approved by a vote of the people, or whether such changes must have the sanction of the Legislature? The people's constitution, so called, was adopted upon the former theory, and contained an express declaration of that doctrine. The landholders' constitution, which had been called pursuant to a law of the Assembly, contained no declaration upon this vital question of difference.

In the convention which formed the present constitution it was proposed to adopt the provision of the people's constitution. The matter was vehemently discussed, and referred to a committee, consisting of E. R. Potter, James F. Simmons, and Nehemiah R. Knights. The chairman, E. R. Potter, had issued a pamphlet upon the Rhode Island question, in which he had said : "The more we consider these things, the more reason we shall see in the old-fashioned doctrine, that a change of government can only take place in one of two ways — legally, with the consent of the existing government, or by a revolution, brought about by force, or the fear of force." The provision in its present form was adopted. The law and order party, of which this constitution was "the crowning work," held that the consent of the existing government made a change legal.

The chief justice argues that this provision of the Declaration of Rights is changed by the subsequent provision for a mode of amendment of the constitution. To this position insuperable objections exist.

First. If that provision for amendment is construed so as to limit and change the declaration of the Bill of Rights, and we are to consider both, which is to prevail? That question is answered by the constitution itself. In case of conflict the Declaration of Rights is to prevail. The language of the constitution immediately preceding this section is as follows : "In order effectually to secure the religious and political freedom established by our venerated ancestors, and to preserve the same for our posterity, we do declare that the essential and unquestionable rights and principles hereinafter mentioned shall be established, maintained, and preserved, and shall be of paramount obligation in all legislative, judicial, and executive proceedings."

Second. As the meaning of the Declaration is clear upon the question, we should construe a provision for amendment made by our wise and good fathers as consistent with it.

Third. As the provision for amendment does not in terms exclude proceedings for a convention, there should be some reason for giving it that effect by implication, as strong as an express declaration would be.

Fourth. It would be an imputation upon the framers of the constitution, which, being such men as the pamphlet describes them to be, they did not deserve, to suppose that they used the language of Washington with a different meaning from that in which he used it. *If they meant that the constitution should be changed only in the special mode, why did they not say so?*

Fifth. The chief justice says (page 46) : " If the declaratory clause, which was offered and rejected in the convention which framed our constitution, had been adopted, we should find it difficult to maintain that the special provision is exclusive and controlling."

That clause was the one contained in the people's constitution, which affirmed, in substance, the right of the people to change their constitution without a previous act of legislation. The people's constitution, it may be observed in passing, contained a provision for amendment like our own, except that it required only a majority vote of the people to effect the amendment. The chief justice admits that such provision for amendment would not overrule the declaratory clause in the Bill of Rights ; so, doubtless, thought Mr. Dorr and the men who framed and voted for that constitution. The declaratory clause in our constitution affirmed the right of the people to change it by any explicit and authentic act. The usual mode of changing a constitution in this country by legislation, convention, and popular vote, is beyond all question an explicit and authentic act of the whole people. Why should this more limited expression of the right of the people to reform their institutions be further limited by the provision for amendment, if the larger right expressed in the people's constitution was confessedly not thus limited ?

The provision of the Bill of Rights is not referred to in the opinion nor in the report of the committee of the General

Assembly. It did not occur to the judges, it is to be presumed, in the conference which the pamphlet implies that they held, and we have not their opinion upon it. We have, however, the opinion of the pamphlet.

It says the section declares that the existing constitution remains obligatory till changed by an explicit and authentic act of the whole people. "There are two requirements here: first, the act must be authentic; and second, it must be the the act of the whole people. To meet these requirements, the act must be performed under the sanction of the law, for otherwise it cannot be legally authenticated, nor be the act of the whole people, if any portion of them dissent. The vote of any number less than all cannot be the vote of the whole people, even in contemplation of law, unless it is legally and constitutionally given. It is not enough, therefore, that the change is effected under an act of the General Assembly, unless the act is constitutional. An unconstitutional statute is a nullity. We are thus brought back to the very question which I have already so fully argued, namely, whether an act which purports to provide for a change of the constitution in any manner other than that which is prescribed in the special provision is constitutional. I maintain, for reasons which I need not repeat, that such an act, being inconsistent with the special provision, is unconstitutional and void. It follows that the only mode in which our constitution can be changed by 'an explicit and authentic act of the whole people' is the mode prescribed in the special provision."

We give the pamphlet the benefit of its careful and full reasoning. The assumption that the permission for amendment is exclusive and controlling, has no basis, as the examination of the pamphlet shows. But assume, for the sake of the argument, that such an implication can be derived from it; and assume that the declarations in the Bill of Rights and other provisions do not negative such implication, resting, as it does, on inference merely, from the words of a provision which does not stand alone in granting powers of action in this matter; and assume that it is the only mode by which, under the constitution, the right of the people to alter their constitution can be exercised.

What follows? This declaration in the Bill of Rights, in its very first section: "That the basis of our political system is the right of the people to make and alter their constitution of government, but that the constitution which at any time exists, till changed by an explicit and authentic act of the whole people, is sacredly obligatory upon all." And the preamble to the whole declaration, that the rights declared in it "shall be of paramount obligation on all legislative, judicial, and executive proceedings," this preamble and section are both, so far as this fundamental right is concerned, absolutely useless and without meaning. They confer or secure no rights, according to the pamphlet, except those otherwise conferred and secured in the provision for legislative proposition for amendments of the constitution. If that clause is exclusive and controlling, this constitutional guaranty of the great American right of self-government by the people is nothing, in effect, but blank paper. The right outside the constitution is extinguished, the pamphlet also claims, by the same exclusive and controlling provision. This makes the whole Bill of Rights, in this respect, a simple piece of useless absurdity. If the framers of the constitution were such men as the pamphlet describes them to be, would they have engaged in such an imposition and mockery upon the people of the State? Shall we now gravely say that the constitution has precisely the meaning it would have had, had not the careful language of Washington been chosen as its corner-stone? There is such a thing, the pamphlet says, as the *reductio ad absurdum*, " showing that a thing must be erroneous because it is absurd." Simple common-sense will prefer to continue in those words their natural and admitted meaning, before the adoption of the constitution, the same meaning afterward and forevermore.

What has been ever the spirit and meaning of the Rhode Island fathers? The pamphlet says: "Hitherto Rhode Island has led her sisters oftener than she has followed them. It is her glory that she began her career by leading the world." With her sister States she formed the Union; with them she declared in that solemn act her doctrine of liberty and law. It has no uncertain sound. Let her sons in all positions and capacities be true to that great inheritance. She said, through the convention of 1790, "That all power is naturally vested in and consequently derived from the people; that magistrates, therefore, are their trustees and agents, and at all times amenable to them. And that powers of government may be resumed by the people whensoever it shall become necessary to their happiness."

The chief justice, to-day, instead of drawing from these fountains, holds doctrines for which political analogies existed only in the early and untaught States in the slave-holding portions of the country. A number of their constitutions contained provisions vesting power in their legislatures to change their constitutions without a vote of the people, though they never denied the power of the people, in convention assembled, through its acts and a popular vote, to change them. Those States and constitutions were: South Carolina, 1790; Delaware, 1792, 1831; Georgia, 1798; Missouri, 1820; Arkansas, 1836; Florida, 1838. There have been no others. Such power in legislatures has vanished with the growth of American liberty and intelligence.

The people of Rhode Island will not be pleased that their chief justice has in his rhetoric "blazoned in letters of living light" South Carolina's act of secession. They remember, as does every American, the hallowed words of Webster, uttered in blessing and not in derision, as he read upon his country's flag, "Everywhere spread all over in characters of living light, blazing on all its ample folds as they float over the sea and over the land and in every wind under the whole heavens, that other sentiment dear to every true American heart, Liberty and Union, now and forever, one and inseparable."

ARTICLE IV., SECTION 10.

The provision that "The General Assembly shall continue to exercise the powers they have heretofore exercised, unless prohibited in this constitution," includes the legislative power of calling a constitutional convention, which power it had theretofore exercised on four occasions, unless that power is prohibited in the constitution.

The origin, historically and literally, of this provision may be briefly stated. The People's Convention, so called, framed a constitution in October, 1841. The Landholders' Convention, called under an act of the General Assembly, met in November, 1841, and adjourned to February, 1842, when it completed its work. In December, 1841, the vote was taken on the People's Convention, when its supporters claimed that it had been adopted. In March, 1842, the vote was taken on the Landholders' Convention, and it was rejected by about eight hundred majority on a vote of about fifteen thousand. The theory of the people's constitution was in accordance with the usual distribution of power and declaration of rights in other State constitutions. In that convention a learned man in political lore was the leading mind, T. W. Dorr. The landholders' constitution contained largely the same division of powers and similar declarations of rights. It differed in two essential particulars pertinent to the present subject. It contained no declaration of the right of the people to change the constitution. And it did contain (in contrast to the provision in the people's constitution concerning the powers to be retained by the General Assembly) an express statement that "The General Assembly shall continue to exercise the judicial power, the power of visiting corporations, and all other powers they have heretofore exercised not inconsistent with this constitution."

In the convention of 1842, called in June, elected in August, and convened in September of that year, there was some change in the membership compared with the Landholders' Convention. An attempt had been made to inaugurate the people's constitution, and the officers elected under it. The general government had been appealed to by the charter government, and had promised to support it. Martial law had been declared at the same time the convention act was passed. It was suspended while the voting for delegates was taking place. The convention was of one political party. Mr. Simmons, Chief Justice Durfee, and William Sprague were of the new members of that convention.

The delegation from Providence to the Landholders' Convention had been Joseph Veazie, Thomas W. Dorr, William C. Barker, Hezekiah Willard, Oliver Johnson, Thaddeus Curtis. The delegates to the new convention were Charles F. Tillinghast, Charles Jackson, William Tallman, James Fenner, Isaac Thurber, Nehemiah R. Knight. The former, it is believed, were suffrage men; the latter moderate law and order men. Or if Gov. Fenner is to be considered of a more extreme type, it is to be remembered that he wore the suffrage badge in the ox-roasting suffrage procession of 1841. William Sprague had voted for the people's constitution, and had since been elected United States senator by the law and order party.

With this change in circumstances, and in the personal memberships of the convention, it will not be supposed that the convention would make its constitution any less of the old Rhode Island type. It therefore provided that "all the powers they have heretofore exercised" (the most simple and comprehensive term) should be continued to the General Assembly. In the landholders' constitution it named two powers and added "all other." The very specification, according to a usual rule of construction, might limit the general word to those of the kind enumerated. The reservation was no longer "not inconsistent with" (that is, open to argument and opinion), but "unless prohibited," which is strong, emphatic, and means something clear and definite to the public mind. It can be easily imagined that Mr. Simmons, with his determination to maintain, so far as possible, the old order of things, might have suggested these changes of expression. He did not forget the power of the Assembly to call conventions.

In deference to the construction of the phrases distributing power in other constitutions, the judicial power has been by the court taken from the Assembly, notwithstanding the tenth section, its origin and construction. The construction claimed for the word "prohibited" in the pamphlet, not only deprives the Assembly of a great and accustomed right, but it is reached by putting a different construction from that put everywhere else upon the same amendment provision in a constitution. Its supporters have at once to contend against our State and most of the other States. In such a contest the result in the long run is inevitable.

PENNSYLVANIA DECISIONS.

That of the Supreme Court of Pennsylvania in Wells v. Bain (75 Pa. St. 46) was quoted in the article. Not a word of it meets the eye of the reader of the pamphlet. It is explicit enough, that the modes of legal change are two. *First*, The mode provided in the existing constitution. *Second*, "A law, as the instrumental process of raising the body for revision, and conveying to it the power of the people." Fuller quotation may be found in the article. The distinction between the two methods was fully considered by the Court. But the argument or points of counsel are not given. The counsel were R. S. Ashurst, J. E Gowen, B. H. Brewster (now attorney-general of the United States), on one side, and C. R. Buckalew, W. H. Armstrong, and G. W. Biddle, on the other. The presumption is that everything was argued, at least everything that was decided elaborately by the Court. The Court do not say, as the pamphlet does, that "the lawfulness of the convention was assumed"; on the contrary, it elaborately argues and discusses the lawfulness of the convention, and sustains it.

The pamphlet says of the judge's opinion in Wood's appeal: "For the theory is identical with one of Judge Bradley's theories, which I have considered, and which I think I have shown to be chimerical." We will now quote some of the reasoning and learning of the judge, and see where the chimera is. The positions that the judge considers are these: "There is no power given by the present constitution to the Legislature authorizing such a proceeding. There is a different method provided by the constitution, by which it may be amended, and, therefore, upon well-recognized principles of law, the legal conclusion arises that no other exists." The argument of counsel he states as follows: "It is urged, and with much apparent force, that because the constitution, in the tenth article 'of amendments,' provides a certain and carefully defined way for amending the fundamental law, the well-recognized legal maxim ordinarily applies to the construction of deeds and written instruments, as well as acts of legislation, '*Expressio unius est exclusio alterius,*' leads to the fixed legal presumption that no amendment can, under the constitution, be made to it, except in the way thus specially provided."

His own reasoning is in part thus stated : "Custom and usage have also been allowed to aid in interpreting acts of Parliament, 'and that exposition,' says Lord Coke, 'shall be preferred which is applied by constant use and experience.' It is by no means certain that the maxim alluded to should find any favor as a general rule of interpretation of an instrument like a constitution, which must of necessity deal in generalities ; but at all events, if so applied, it must in all such cases be considered as overcome by any established or common usage or understanding, indicating a different conclusion."

His conclusion is : "Turning now to the history of the gov ernment of the various States, for the purpose of discovering what the usage in such cases has been, we find the practice has been so frequent and uniform as clearly to indicate what the common understanding of the people, lawyer and laymen, has been in regard to this question."

After great research, he adds : "The question whether the calling of a constitutional convention was a legal exercise of power by the Legislature, should now be considered by all judicial tribunals as settled so firmly as a part of the common law of our government, that any attempt to disturb it would savor more of revolution than legitimacy." This is the only passage from the opinion quoted in the article. The pamphlet terms it "judicial thunder."

The pamphlet says : "Judge Bradley says the opinion of the inferior court was sustained by the Supreme Court. This is an error." This statement is a multiform error. The article did not say so. If it had, it would have been correct.

The Supreme Court in Wood's appeal say : "The calling of a convention and regulating its action by law is not forbidden in the constitution. It is a conceded manner through which the people may exercise the right reserved in the Bill of Rights," and thus sustains the decision of the Court on the point now at issue. The opinion re-enforces that given in Wells v. Bain.

That case of Wells v. Bain was in the Supreme Court, as stated in the article. The Supreme Court in Wells v. Bain gave the same judgment as to the lawfulness of the convention that was given by the inferior court in Wood's appeal.

The further assertion in the pamphlet "that the lower court had promulgated a wild and extravagant theory in regard to the power of constitutional conventions, and that the Supreme Court had dissected and demolished that theory in a manner which, to say the least, will not add to the reputation of its author as a wise and trustworthy guide on questions of constitutional law," is an error. The decision of Stowe, J., was that the convention was right in disregarding the limitations sought to be imposed upon its power, both as to what it should propose to change in the present constitution, and how the proposal should be submitted to the people for their adoption or rejection. Another question as to the right of the convention to repeal an act of legislation, it did not decide because "immaterial" to the parties before it.

The facts out of which these cases arose were that the Assembly by law in 1841 submitted to the people the question of assembling a convention. And the vote of the people was in the affirmative. The Assembly of 1842 enacted some limitations and made certain provisions in regard to the action of the convention. The convention appointed by ordinance a board of inspectors of election in Philadelphia, different from the board appointed by existing law. The Supreme Court enjoined the board appointed by the convention from acting under their appointment. After the constitution had been adopted, the case of Wood's appeal came before the court. They said the matter was no longer open to judicial cognizance, but proceeded to give an extra-judicial opinion, arraigning as illegal the alleged purpose of the convention to adopt a constitution without submitting it to the people. They decide in conclusion that there is nothing "which can justify an assumption that a convention so called, constituted, organized and limited, can take from the people their sovereign right to ratify or reject a constitution or ordinance framed by it, or can infuse present life and vigor into its work before its adoption by the people." Wood's appeal, 76 Penn. St. p. 75.

While the convention, through its committee, advised submission to the injunction of the court, upon reassembling, it resolved, by a vote of seventy-seven to seven, that "the convention was called by authority of the people, as determined by their vote under the act of 1871, declaring that a convention shall be called to amend the constitution of this Commonwealth, and this was a mandate to the Legislature, which that body was not at liberty to disobey or modify."

And by vote of sixty-three to thirteen, the convention further resolved, in substance, that the constitution had reserved the right to modify the government, and "excepted it out of the general powers of government, and declared that such right shall remain inviolate." "It is not in the power of any department of an existing government to limit or control the power of the convention, and that the convention, subject only to the constitution of the United States, is answerable only to the people." The courts and the "convention filled with the best men in the State"* concur (however they differ as to the respective sphere of the Legislature and convention) that a convention is constitutionally holden in Pennsylvania, under a constitution that provides for amendment like our own, and contains no special provision for a convention. Neither courts nor convention, no one, in short, who had the responsibility of judgment, then held that the provision for amendment limited or prohibited the exercise of power expressed in the Bill of Rights. A Bill of Rights in that State means what it says, and is not set aside by an inference as to the meaning of another clause. If the people of one State may legally and constitutionally proceed in the accustomed manner, and notwithstanding the provisions for legislative amendment, why not Rhode Island also in a manner included in the terms used in her Bill of Rights?

---

* The opinion says: "The act opened a wide door to men of all parties, and filled the convention with the best men in the State."

THE OPINION AND ACTION OF JUDGES, JURISTS, AND STATESMEN IN MASSACHUSETTS.

The opinion of the Massachusetts judges, and the examination of it in the article, and the opinions of leading jurists of that State, in its convention of 1853, as quoted in the article, are both easily disposed of in the pamphlet; the latter by absolute silence. The examination of the opinion in the article, to determine its true meaning, the author of the pamphlet seeks to dispose of by simply saying, "Judge Bradley tries to explain it away; I do not think he succeeds."

The chief justice quotes one of the questions and one of the answers. That question propounded to the Massachusetts judges was: "Can any specific and particular amendment or amendments be made in any other manner than that prescribed in the ninth article of the amendments adopted in 1820?" Their answer was: "Under and pursuant to the existing constitution there is no authority given by any reasonable construction or necessary implication by which any specific and particular amendment or amendments of the constitution can be made in any other manner than that prescribed in the ninth article of the amendments adopted in 1820." That is, a legislative mode of amendment, created by the constitution, does not authorize another mode. This is all that the pamphlet quotes. As to the question here pending, whether any other mode of change may coexist, whether changes can be made through a convention, the validity of such a proceeding ultimately seems to be implied in the other question and answer.

"*Second.* Whether, if the Legislature should call a convention of delegates for the purpose of making a specific revision of the constitution in certain departments, that convention would have any power to go beyond these specific amendents proposed by the terms of the vote calling the convention?"

Ans. "If the Legislature should submit to the people the expediency of calling a convention to revise or alter the constitution in any specified part thereof, and the people should, by the terms of their vote, decide to call a convention, the delegates would derive their whole authority and commission from such vote, and would have no right, under the same, to propose amendments in other parts of the constitution not specified."

The pamphlet, after quoting the first question and answer says, "That is all of the opinion which is pertinent. It is short, but in Mercutio's phrase, 'it is enough.' Judge Bradley cannot parry it. It leaves him without any ground to stand upon but this : That though an amendment cannot be constitutionally made in the form of an amendment, in any other than the prescribed mode, it can be constitutionally made independently of that mode, if you only put it in the form of a new constitution, and call it reconstruction. My opinion is that the grand old Massachusetts chief justice would have made short work with that argument, if he had had occasion to consider it."

One of Chief Justice Shaw's colleagues, who signed the opinion, probably understood it as well as the author of the pamphlet. Judge Morton, who with his son, the present chief justice, was a member of the convention, said, "If the people choose to adopt what we submit to them it then becomes authority." This is the question submitted to our judges. Joel Parker, formerly chief justice of New Hampshire, then a professor at the Cambridge Law School, said, " I believe this convention to have been lawfully assembled."

He further says : —

" Is not this mode of amending the constitution, which is prescribed in the constitution in express terms, perfectly consistent with the other mode, by a convention of delegates? There is no antagonism between the two modes. The people say by their constitution, ' We will have a convenient mode by which this instrument can be amended without a convention ; and we will therefore embody a provision that the opinion of two successive Legislatures that the constitution ought to be amended shall be submitted to us for our action without the expense of a convention.' This is all very well ; but does it exclude the idea that there is any other mode? Does it exclude the idea that a convention may be holden, when there is nothing antagonistical between the two modes? By no means. Sir, I do not stand alone in this opinion. I am supported in it by eminent writers on constitutional law. I will read an extract from Mr. Rawle's Treatise on the Constitution, the work of a jurist of well-known reputation, and one whose opinions are entitled to high respect. He says : —

"'The laws of one legislature may be repealed by another legislature, and the power to repeal them cannot be withheld by the power that enacted them. So the people may, on the same principle, at any time, alter or abolish the constitution they have framed. This has been frequently and peaceably done by several of these States since 1776. If a particular mode of affecting such alterations has been agreed on, it is most convenient to adhere to it, but it is not exclusively binding.'

"There is the doctrine laid down distinctly. If a particular mode has been designated by which this may be done, it is convenient to adhere to it, but it is not exclusively binding. It may be done in other modes; and the mode by which it is to be done at the present time is by the action of this convention."

Judge Sprague of the United States District Court, formerly a member of the United States Senate from Maine, said : " I agree with them (Judges Morton and Parker), that the act of the Legislature, by virtue of which the convention was assembled, was to be their guide. It was the charter, the organic law of that body, under which they must act, and they had no right to go beyond its true meaning . . . whether it be considered as deriving its force merely from the Legislature, or also from adoption by the people." And Rufus Choate, then attorney-general of Massachusetts, a coadjutor in all things political with Webster, a member of the same bar, that of Salem, with Chief Justice Shaw, speaking of the power of the Legislature, under the constitution, to pass an act regulating the mode of electing delegates to the convention, said : " To my judgment it is perfectly clear that they had, and which nobody has yet called in question." Henry Wilson, the life-long senator of Massachusetts and Vice-President of the United States, said (Debates in the Massachusetts Convention, 1853, Vol. I. p. 179) : —

" Whether the act of 1852 has any warrant in the constitution
or not, it has the authority of precedent, the precedent of
the convention of 1780 that framed the constitution, and of
the convention of 1820, by which it was revised. Thirty-one
State constitutions have been formed, thirty-two conventions
have been held in nineteen States for the revision of their
organic laws. These sixty-three conventions, running through
seventy-seven years, have almost uniformly been held in accordance with the provisions of legislative enactments. This mode
to ascertain the sense of the people has become the practice of
the States, — the practice alike of States having provisions for
thus taking the sense of the people, and of States having no
such provision. This mode has become the fixed practice of
our political system ; it is common law ; it is peculiarly American. Mr. Webster characterized it as the 'American principle.' The act of 1852 is sustained by the almost uniform
precedents of the conventions which framed the constitution of
the United States, and the constitutions of the several States,
and of the conventions which have been called to revise the
constitutions of the States."

It is remarkable that in the long debate in the convention no
reference is made to the opinion of the Court, except by Mr.
Hallett, who quotes it for the position that the convention derives its authority from the vote of the people. What these
men and their compeers said and thought and did upon this
question in Massachusetts was set forth in the article. These
facts the pamphlet — professing to answer everything — does not
notice. One of two things is evident : either these jurists of
Massachusetts thought the opinion was as claimed in the article
and was right, or was as claimed in the pamphlet and was
wrong.

It was intended, in those amendatory clauses of the Massachusetts constitution, that it should not provide a mode for a
general revision of the constitution. It was intended to be
limited to the amendments, in the original sense of the word,
which should be necessary from time to time. This meaning is
plainly intended in the words used ; they are, " specific and particular amendments." Those, of themselves, to a fair mind,

would not include a new constitution. The framers of that constitution thought, as usual, their work would need nothing but amendment. If it should, the way was open, in the history of the State and the country, to make such revision. Once, in the history of the State, a new constitution has been proposed by the Legislature and rejected by the people. Twice had conventions been called. The constitution framed by the first was approved by the people; the second was then engaged at its work. All this is made plain by what was said in the Convention Proceedings, 417 : "Mr. Webster repeated the grounds on which he made the proposition. It occurred to the committee that, with the experience which we had had of the constitution, there was little probability that, after the amendments which should now be adopted, there would ever be any occasion for great changes. No revision of its general principles would be necessary, and the alterations which should be called for by a change of circumstances would be limited and specific. It was therefore the opinion of the committee *that no provision for a revision of the whole constitution was expedient, and the only question was in what manner it should be provided that particular amendments might be obtained.* It was a natural course, and conformable to analogy and precedent in some degree, that every proposition for amendment should originate in the Legislature under certain guards, and be sent out to the people. The question then arose, what guards should be provided? It was thought proper to provide that an amendment should not be proposed and sent out to the people under the influence of a popular excitement. To prevent this they proposed to require the repeated assent of the Legislature; and the question, in the mean time, would be, in some measure, tried by the people, who would express their opinions in the next election. This was one of the guards which they proposed, and another was, that the measure should be assented to by more than a bare majority of the two houses." Mr. Pickman, who closed the debate, said "he did not consider it a question what power should be vested in the people, but what power should be vested in the Legislature. He agreed that the people are the sovereigns of the country, and that a majority must control the will of the people. But the question now was, what powers should be given to the Legislature." Did Mr. Webster understand the meaning of the clause he helped to prepare? There had been, previous to his time, express provisions for calling a constitutional convention.

MR. WEBSTER'S POSITION ON THIS QUESTION.

What Mr. Webster said in his argument in the Rhode Island case, and what he submitted to the world in the last volume of his works (and thereby intended, presumably, to leave as an expression of opinion, and not merely as the argument of an advocate), was quoted in the article. The pamphlet gives its version of it. A quarter of the space would have sufficed to have quoted it, and then its readers could have formed some opinion as to the truth of the assertion in the pamphlet, " That Judge Bradley claims that Mr. Webster is authority. The claim is simply conjectural." We quote, as in the article, the language of Mr. Webster. None of it is quoted in the pamphlet. The constitution of New York contained a provision for amendment similar to our own. It contained no provision under which any one claimed that the Legislature had power to call a convention, except the general grant of legislative power. Mr. Webster said, " One of the most recent laws for taking the will of the people in any State is the law of 1845 of the State of New York. It begins by recommending to the people to assemble in their several election districts, and proceed to vote for delegates to a convention. If you will take the pains to read that act, it will be seen that New York regarded it as an ordinary exercise of legislative power. It applies all the penalties for fraudulent voting, as in other elections. It punishes false oaths, as in other cases. Certificates of the proper officers were to be held conclusive, and the will of the people was, in this respect, collected essentially in the same manner, supervised by the same officers, under the same guards against force and fraud, collusion and misrepresentation, as are usual in voting for State or United States officers."

"We see, therefore, from the commencement of the government under which we live down to this late act of the State of New York, one uniform current of law, of precedent, and of practice, all going to establish the point that changes in government are to be brought about by the will of the people, assembled under such legislative provisions as may be necessary to ascertain that will truly and authentically."

The pamphlet argues that when he said this he did not believe that the act of New York was constitutional. And yet he takes it as an illustration of the American method of changing our State governments. If it fatally departed from "the current of law, of precedent, and of practice," in Mr. Webster's opinion as it does in the opinion of the author of the pamphlet, and that to a ridiculous extent, as he claims, could Mr. Webster have described it as a part of that current? But the language is plain enough.

Omitting all of this, the pamphlet quotes at length what Mr. Webster said in the same argument about the power of the people to limit themselves in their constitution, and the care they had taken "to secure what they had established against hasty changes by simple majorities." He instances only the provision in the constitution of the United States. Two things it may be well for the reader to remember: one that Mr. Webster cites and the constitution contains provisions for amendment through legislation and through conventions. These two methods exist in the United States, and in the States; the author of the pamphlet has never been able to perceive that the power to change through convention is coexistent with the power to change through legislation. When the mind is once open to a realizing sense of this undoubted historic fact, the whole counter argument, to quote it, "vanishes like a vapor."

Another fact to be borne in mind here is the different nature and powers of the general government and of the State governments. Mr. Webster has stated that difference in terms quoted in the article. In short, that the general government is one of specified powers, and that the State legislatures have all usual powers, subject only to the limitations imposed by the State constitutions or the United States constitution.

Again it may be observed that Mr. Webster points out only the provisions preventing hasty action by requiring a majority merely in initiating amendments. The final action on the question of changing the constitution of the United States is by a mere majority either of the legislature or the convention. It is not submitted to the people as are changes in a State constitution. The United States were a combination of States, and not one state, when the constitution was formed. What illustrations Mr. Webster takes from its provisions for changes are not so instructive as what he says upon the mode of changing State constitutions.

We will quote from the same speech what he says upon changes in State constitutions : —

"Yet there is hardly one that has not altered its constitution ; and it has been done by conventions called by the Legislature as an ordinary exercise of legislative power. Now what State ever altered its constitution in any other mode? What alteration has ever been brought in, forced in, or got in any how, by resolutions of mass meetings and then by applying force? In what State has an assembly calling itself the people, convened without law, without authority, without qualifications, without certain officers, with no oaths, securities or sanctions of any kind, met and made a constitution, and called it a constitution of the State? There must be some authentic mode of ascertaining the will of the people, else all is anarchy."

Again he says, "What do I contend for? I say that the will of the people must prevail when it is ascertained ; but there must be some legal and authentic mode of ascertaining that will, and then the people may make what government they please."

Again, "But the law and the constitution, the whole system of American institutions, do not contemplate a case in which a resort will be necessary to proceedings *aliunde*, or outside of the law and the constitution, for the purpose of amending the frame of government. They go on the idea that the States are all republican, that they are all representative in their forms, and that these popular governments in each State, the annually created creatures of the people, will give all proper facilities and neces-

sary aids to bring about changes which the people may judge
necessary in the constitutions. They take this ground and
act on no other supposition. They assume that the popular
will, in all particulars, will be accomplished. And history has
proved that the presumption is well founded.

"This, may it please your Honors, is the view I take of what
I have called the American system. These are the methods of
bringing about changes in government."

Referring to the passage quoted in it, the pamphlet observes:
'I want the reader to study these pregnant sentences. Mr.
Webster says the people limit themselves. He says they
secure the forms of government which they establish, from
hasty changes, by simple majorities. He tell us that this is
their great conservative principle. But how do they secure
their forms of government from hasty changes by simple majorities? He shows how, by referring to the provision," etc.

"Is it not clear then, that his meaning is, that the people
secure their forms of government from hasty changes by simple
majorities, by prescribing modes of amendment which require
the consent of more than simple majorities? This is evidently
what he means. He mentions no other way, and so far as I
know, there was no other way in which such security was made
in any State constitution."

This assertion is of two things. First, that Mr. Webster
means that the people secure their form of government by prescribing modes of amendment which require the consent of more
than simple majorities. Second, that in fact there is no other
way in which such security is obtained in any State constitution.
The inference as to Mr. Webster's meaning has no foundation
in what he has said, except that more than a majority of a legislature is sometimes required to initiate proceedings and thus
to prevent haste or surprise. Our constitution does not contain
that provision. Mr. Webster never said that a constitution
may require more than a majority of the popular vote to make
a change. The provision for amendment in our constitution
requires three fifths.

In what sense does Mr. Webster use the word "people" in the
passages quoted from him? He means the majority who repre-

sent the whole in the vote. He never was so un-American as to claim that a minority could prevail when questions of amendment or change of constitution were submitted to the vote of the people.

Mr. Webster said in the Massachusetts convention, 1820, page 407, " He knew no principle that could prevent a majority, even a bare majority of the people from altering the constitution."

The pamphlet says that Mr. Webster mentions no other mode of securing the form of government from change than " by requiring the consent of more than a majority." Mr. Webster certainly nowhere mentions that mode as to be applied on a vote by the people.

But the chief justice says : " So far as I know, there was no other way in which such security was made in any State constitution."

We are brought now to a question of fact. The collection of State constitutions made by the Hon. Ben : Perley Poore, pursuant to an act of Congress, shows that there have been eighty-four State constitutions in force in this country. In but two of those is there a provision requiring more than a majority vote of the people to adopt either an amendment or a change of the constitution. One of these constitutions is that of New Hampshire of 1792. The other is the present constitution of Rhode Island. In the light of these facts, what are we to think of the knowledge of the chief justice on the subject as declared by himself? And what becomes of his interpretation of the meaning of Mr. Webster's language? Who, to use the expression of the pamphlet, " Empties that language of its significance "?

CHARGE OF THE ELDER CHIEF JUSTICE DURFEE HOW TO BE CONSIDERED.

The pamphlet quotes, in its conclusion, from a paper purporting to be the memoranda of a charge to the grand jury in 1843, by the elder Chief Justice Durfee.

It has often been the pleasure of this writer to render tribute

to the high power of that chief justice, especially to his philosophic and poetic cast of mind, and to the manly impulses of
his nature. But, like all men, the chief justice had his limitation. No one ever claimed for him great learning in the law.
The pamphlet has recalled events occurring further back than
the lifetime of a generation, and yet as vivid as yesterday in
the memory of the actors.

There was occasion, at the time, for the writer to express his
opinion of that magistrate, then not long deceased. The House
had passed a resolution declaring the seats of all the judges
vacant. This resolution came to the Senate. Every vote of the
majority was needed. The writer, having one vote, said that he
could not concur in such a resolution unless there could be found
a man to take the place of chief justice, who was either, like the
late chief justice, a man of such intellectual power that he
could understand a case when it had been well argued on both
sides and decide it correctly, or a man like the then Chief
Justice Greene, whose legal learning and judicial habit of mind
would usually enable him to decide rightly. This opinion
was by no means singular; it was the common understanding of the bar at the time. What is more, the chief himself
knew and acknowledged the limitations referred to. Mr. Ames,
conversing upon the subject once in the court house, as this
writer distinctly remembers, said, after expressing strongly his
opinion as to this deficiency in learning: "The chief justice
says himself, that he often feels out of place on the bench because he is called upon to administer a science which he has not
studied." Constitutional questions are historic questions. No
man's intuitions or reasoning are sufficient for them. The meaning of terms in an instrument depends upon usage. Not to
know the usage is not to know the meaning. Hence Daniel
Webster's argument (which has just been quoted) as to the
American methods of changing the constitution is largely a
statement of historic facts.

Thus much as to the learning of the elder chief justice, and
the need of it on such a question. A striking instance of want
of knowledge in the present chief justice as to the usual constitutional requirement of a majority, and of a consequent error

in judgment and misinterpretation of Mr. Webster's language, we have just seen. There was another serious difficulty in the early chief justice, growing out of the large and powerful impulses of his nature. His feelings would lead his judgment. Witness two instances: One in his conduct in the Dorr trial, in which, as we see by the quotations from the report, he was first and last and all the time of the opinion that all the members of one political party should be excluded from the panel of the jury. This is a natural opinion for an outsider. But a jurist, who understands the nature of a jury trial in our history, could not take such a view. Judges Staples and Brayton did not concur with him. Even the *Journal* did not.

In a similar English case, to use the phrase of the popular historian, a Tory sheriff wrongfully selected a Tory jury. One party has the administration of the laws entirely in its hands, and can wield it for the destruction of its political opponents; now, perhaps, in trials for treason; now, in trials for libel. It is of such proceedings that the great advocate Erskine uttered his words of wisdom and fire.

Witness again the philosophic and poetic and eloquent charge of the late chief justice to the grand jury at Bristol, in March, 1842. The conclusion the elder chief justice reaches in his own mind, and with which he would terrify the public mind, is that if the government should be changed by the adoption of the people's constitution, Rhode Island would cease to be one of the United States. Congress would not recognize the State. The Supreme Court would not recognize her. Her constitution would be of no more value in the courts of the Union than so much blank parchment. He proceeds: —

"What becomes of the public property of all sorts? your court houses? your jails? your public records? public treasury bonds and securities of all sorts which belong to the present corporate Rhode Island, and to her only, and can pass from her only by her legislative consent? What become of the actions now pending on the dockets of every court in this State, bills of indictment for crimes committed or that may be committed? What becomes of your State prison and your convicts, from the wilful murderer to the petty thief? What becomes of your corporations of all sorts? of your corporate towns and their records? Nay, are there not questions touching life, liberty, and individual property? I dare go no further; perhaps I have already gone too far. But whatever answer may be given to these questions (and answered they must ultimately be in the Supreme Court of the Union), the bare fact that these questions must be raised, tried, and decided is sufficient to send a thrill of horror through the heart of every man, woman, and child in this State."

What an utter want here of practical wisdom! What a want of judicial wisdom! Did not the chief justice with his colleagues shortly afterwards decide that the political question as to the existence of a constitution upon which such title depends is one for the political and not the judicial department of the government?

Again, the notes of this charge to the grand jury in 1843 were not considered by their author or his son and biographer as sufficiently complete for publication in the collection of his works, notwithstanding the importance of the subject. A charge to a grand jury is not a judgment of a court. Judgments are valuable and make the safe basis upon which society rests, because they are the result of contending argument. The opinion of any man without such examination of both sides of a question is not a judicial one, though it may have come from a judge. To transfer to the personal opinion of one holding judicial office the weight attached to the opinion judicially formed, is to encourage that most dangerous tendency in a judge to decide cases without regard to the argument of the parties. This is such a failure to perform the duties of the office that the judge who thus conducts himself is entitled to have his seat declared vacant

Did the elder chief justice live in our day, the present writer believes that he would not have expressed the opinion attributed to him, and that a man of his high qualities and powers would not have approved of the pamphlet before us.

The memoranda before us seem to show in one portion of them that the early chief justice thought a provision for amendment was exclusive of all other modes of change. And yet when he comes to his final proposition, he uses language which would recognize other legal modes of change. He says, "or change of government, effected without pursuing a legal course." A change through a convention and act of legislation and vote of the people is a legal course, and therefore comes within the language of the charge. If its author meant to include any legal course, there is no conflict. If he meant to say that the amendment was the only legal mode of change, then there is such conflict. Now let us test the practical wisdom of such an opinion, if we construe it as the pamphlet does. The memorandum says: "Once establish it as constitutional law in the Union that an article providing for the amendment of a constitution may be disregarded, or a change of government effected, without pursuing a legal course, and the last trumpet has sounded, and the day of doom has come to our political institutions." Such a doctrine has been established law in New York, and Pennsylvania, and Missouri, Tennessee, Georgia, Louisiana, Arkansas, and Texas, and even in Massachusetts, and throughout the country; indeed was proclaimed by the advocates for Rhode Island, John Whipple and Daniel Webster, in the Supreme Court of the United States only five years after the delivery of the charge. It was acted upon by the general government in the restoration of the seceding States. Did the last trump sound and the day of doom come? Let us put aside rhetoric and rely upon practical wisdom in the affairs of government. Practical wisdom tests the soundness of political philosophy.

CONCLUSION.

This reply is offered as a contribution towards the knowledge of events in the history of the State, most of the actors in which have departed, and upon which the calm light of history has not yet arisen.

It is offered also as a contribution to the knowledge of what has occurred in other States, bearing on the questions submitted by the Honorable the Senate of the State to the Honorable the Judges of the Supreme Court, concerning a mode of changing the constitution of the State.

Over forty years elapsed, during which the constitutions of American States were changed, through convention and popular vote. Then the method by legislative proposition and popular vote was introduced both at the extreme South and in New England. After over forty years more had elapsed, the commentator on constitutional conventions, having reviewed history, says: "That course," that is, the course of changing a constitution through convention and popular vote, when the existing constitution contained the provision for amendment by legislative provision and popular vote, without providing for a convention, — "that course," he said, "has been pursued, not always without doubt or protest, though generally with the consent of the wise, to which time has commonly added, the acquiescence of all."

More States have followed that course since he wrote than before. Among them the Keystone State and the State which is to be the Empire State of the future. Rhode Island was "first in the fight and last at the feast" of independence and Union. Her people were once ready to fight over the method of changing their constitution. It is to be hoped that they are now ready to unite with their sister States and join in the harmonies of American constitutional liberty and law. For therein are both progress and safety.

www.ingramcontent.com/pod-product-compliance
Lightning Source LLC
Chambersburg PA
CBHW032200010726
47493CB00008BA/2761